BURIED MEMORIES

BURIED MEMORIES

Simon R. Green

SEVERN
HOUSE

First world edition published in Great Britain and the USA in 2021
by Severn House, an imprint of Canongate Books Ltd,
14 High Street, Edinburgh EH1 1TE.

Trade paperback edition first published in Great Britain and the USA in 2022
by Severn House, an imprint of Canongate Books Ltd.

severnhouse.com

British Library Cataloguing-in-Publication Data
A CIP catalogue record for this title is available from the British Library.

ISBN-13: 978-0-7278-9032-0 (cased)
ISBN-13: 978-1-78029-815-3 (trade paper)
ISBN-13: 978-1-4483-0553-7 (e-book)

All Severn House titles are printed on acid-free paper.

MIX
Paper from
responsible sources
FSC® C013056

Typeset by Palimpsest Book Production Ltd.,
Falkirk, Stirlingshire, Scotland.
Printed and bound in Great Britain by
TJ Books, Padstow, Cornwall.

C all me Ishmael. Ishmael Jones.

There was a time when humanity looked up at the night sky and worshipped the stars. When the great sea of space must have seemed a peaceful place, full of awe and wonder, and dreams of what might be out there.

But that was then and this is now.

In 1963, a star fell out of the night and landed in a field, not far from a small English country town. Or, to put it another way, an alien starship came howling down from the outer dark, with its superstructure on fire, and crashed somewhere in the back of beyond. Only this particular falling star didn't just fall; it was pushed. Shot down by its ancient enemy.

Most of the crew died in the impact. The sole survivor had to be rewritten by the ship's transformation machines, right down to its DNA, so it could pass for human. But the machines were damaged in the crash, and when they made the change, they wiped away all memory of who and what I used to be, before I was a man.

I have spent my life working for one secret underground group after another, because only they had the resources to conceal me from an increasingly suspicious world. I had to stay hidden because I haven't aged a day since 1963, because my blood is golden and because I have always known the world isn't ready to know about things like me.

These days, I work for the Organization. I investigate mysteries, protect people from weird threats and solve the occasional murder. Along the way, I fell in love with the delightful Penny Belcourt and now we're partners.

Because I'm only human.

But now, after all these years, a psychic has helped me remember that I wasn't the only one to survive the crash.

There is another. And so I have to go back to the small country town where my memories began, and search for the truth behind all the mysteries that are my life.

Of course, I don't think for one moment it's going to be as simple as that.

ONE

From out of the Past

For most of my underground existence, I never had anywhere I could call home. That's what comes of being born an adult, in the middle of a ploughed field, in the early hours of the morning. Already knowing the world will cage you or kill you, if it finds you.

I spent most of my life going to ground in backstreet hotels, grubby boarding houses and cramped bed-sitting rooms. The kind of place where everybody could be relied on not to know your name, if anyone came around asking questions. I never stayed anywhere long, never used the same name twice and always paid in cash. Forever on the move and under the radar, avoiding all the people and powers who would be far too interested in a man who wasn't really a man.

But then I met the lovely and charming Penny Belcourt – and just like that, my whole life changed. I saved her from a monster, and she rescued me from an empty life. Penny gave me a home, in her flat and in her heart, and I finally had a place where I could feel I belonged.

Penny's charming little abode lies right in the midst of London's most fashionable district, where even a glorified broom closet with no room to swing a cat-o'-nine-tails can cost more than most people make in a lifetime. Penny inherited this little piece of heaven on earth and immediately set about redecorating it to within an inch of its life to better suit her personality. Loud and cheerful and proudly individual. We are talking shocking-pink carpets, wall panels of peacock blue and Imperial Chinese yellow, and assorted technicolour scatter cushions.

To help distract the dazzled eye, the flat also boasts antique furniture, assorted glass sculptures of the Improbable Animals variety, a rubber plant in the corner that somehow continues to thrive despite rampant neglect and disinterest, and a 1920s telephone. I did ask Penny about that last one, but she just smiled brightly and said, 'It's a style thing, darling.' I decided not to pursue the matter. Some areas of human thought remain a mystery to me.

A comfortable setting, for a comfortable life. But it did still worry me, sometimes, that I might be putting Penny in danger by making myself so easy to find. I have enemies – the kind who will never stop searching for me. Enemies who, just like me, only appear to be human.

On this particular evening, Penny and I were sitting snuggled together on the flower-patterned sofa, while we waited for someone to bring us news from my past, from the time before my memories began. Penny was a striking presence in her late twenties, with a pretty face and a great mass of night-dark hair piled up on top of her head. Along with a trim figure, endless enthusiasm and more nervous energy than she knew what to do with. She was wearing designer jeans and her favourite T-shirt: a cartoon of Snoopy in a space helmet, with the legend *An Alien Is Just A Friend I Haven't Met Yet.* I was wearing one of my usual anonymous outfits, guaranteed to ensure no one would ever look at me twice. Because it's bad enough being a target, without having a bullseye painted on your back.

We were waiting for the final results of an investigation I had asked the Organization to carry out on my behalf, to track down the other survivor of the crashed starship. I didn't have the resources to do it myself, and I couldn't afford the kind of attention such questions would be bound to attract. But when a high-up member of the Organization decided he owed me a favour, I knew exactly what to ask for.

The process had taken several weeks, most of which I'd spent so unsettled I'd barely been able to sleep or eat or concentrate. I paced up and down, brooded in armchairs and retreated more and more inside myself. Penny was wise enough to give me my space and did her best to be patient when I couldn't. But earlier that day, the Colonel, my only contact point with the Organization, had phoned to say the report was finally finished and would be delivered into my hands that very evening.

Part of me didn't want to know what was in the file. I couldn't help thinking that the wisest thing to do would be simply to send it back, unread. I'd put a lot of effort into being human. What if the report had uncovered hard evidence that my people were monsters? That we came to Earth for terrible, inhuman reasons? What if my worst nightmare was true after all, and I wasn't what I thought I was?

Now the completed report was finally on its way, Penny had decided she needed to know exactly how much I remembered about my arrival on planet Earth. I went along, to keep her happy – and because I knew I would go crazy with anticipation if I didn't have something to keep me occupied.

'You've spent your whole life investigating mysteries,' said Penny. 'Why wait until now to dig into your past?'

'Because, for a long time, there was only me,' I said. 'Now you're a part of my life, I need to be sure about what you're letting yourself in for. My previous self is not in any way human. It doesn't think or feel like we do, and that makes it dangerous.'

'I don't believe you would ever hurt me,' said Penny.

'I wouldn't,' I said. 'But my other self might.'

'I don't believe that, either,' said Penny. 'Your other self has surfaced in the past, and it always protected me.'

'But we don't know why,' I said. 'If there really is another crash survivor, I need to find out from him whether you might have good reason to be afraid of me.'

She gave me her best reassuring hug. 'I'm your partner, Ishmael; together we investigate mysteries, fight monsters and catch murderers. I'm not going anywhere.'

I didn't tell her I had already decided that if it did turn out I was a threat, I would leave her. To protect her. Even though doing so would break my human heart.

'Have you felt any stirrings from your previous self since you started this excavation into your soul?' said Penny.

'No,' I said. 'So far, it's been all quiet on the alien front.'

'Then it must have decided to sit this one out,' said Penny.

'For its own reasons,' I said.

Penny shook her head. I was never going to be able to convince her, because she hadn't seen the face of the Medusa looking back at her from the bathroom mirror.

'Tell me the very first thing you remember,' said Penny, tucking her legs elegantly beneath her.

'My earliest memories are a mess,' I said. 'Partly because of what the transformation machines did to me, but also because I was born with a head full of downloaded information on how to be human. Dozens of voices, all shouting at once, with no way for me to tell what was important and what could wait.'

'Is that where your name came from?' said Penny. 'It would explain a lot.'

'No,' I said. 'That came later.'

She waited until it became clear I wasn't going to explain, and then she gave me a long-suffering look and pressed on.

'What did your starship look like?'

'It had something of the divine and the infinite about it,' I said slowly. 'A gossamer fortress made of starstuff. Cosmic thistledown, blown across the stars by an astral wind. It looked . . . wrong, lying broken on the ground. It belonged in the heavens, flying on for ever and never having to land.'

'Let's try for something a little more practical,' said Penny. 'How big was it?'

'Like a building that had fallen on its side. It took up most of the field.'

'And no one in Norton Hedley saw something that big crash to Earth?'

'It was the early hours of the morning, and I didn't wait around for anyone to come looking. I could feel the ship watching as I went off and left it behind.'

Penny leaned forward, intrigued. 'The ship was alive?'

'There was some kind of artificial intelligence,' I said. 'Though whether that was the pilot, or the whole ship . . .'

'What else do you remember?' said Penny.

'The ship was ambushed,' I said. 'Shot down, like a bird in flight. Like an angel on the wing.'

'By your enemies – the other aliens?'

'This isn't something I remember,' I said carefully. 'But it's what I've come to believe. Based on dreams and images that haunt me . . . and what little information I've been able to piece together.'

Penny frowned. 'Why didn't your enemies follow you down, to make sure they'd finished all of you off?'

'I don't know. Perhaps they thought that would attract too much attention.'

'And you have no idea who these enemies are?'

'I don't even know who my own people are,' I said. 'Except, of course, they are very definitely not people.'

Penny could tell I was getting uncomfortable talking about myself as though I was somebody else, so she changed the subject.

'What's your last memory of the ship?'

'I saw it burrow down into the earth, burying itself deep so no one would ever be able to find it.'

'Then how are you planning to get to it?' said Penny. 'Pick a field and start digging? Or just stick your head in the ground and call to it, hoping it'll come to you?'

'That ship will never move again,' I said. 'Not with half the local countryside piled on top of it.'

'Then what's your plan?'

'I don't have one. I'm hoping the other crash survivor will have some ideas. He has been living next door to the ship for the last fifty years.'

'Why does it matter so much to you to find your way back to your ship?' said Penny. 'It's not as if you want to go home again. Do you?'

'You know I don't,' I said. 'I need to question the ship's AI about why we came here in the first place, and what we were supposed to be doing here on Earth. Above all, I need some answers about the war going on, out among the stars. Starting with whether my people are the good guys in this conflict.'

Penny looked at me sharply. 'The other aliens shot you down!'

'Maybe they had good reason to.'

'Like what?'

'I don't know! Maybe we weren't supposed to be here.'

Penny looked at me. 'What makes you think your people might not be the good guys?'

'Glimpses of my home world, in dreams I couldn't wake up from. Looking into the face of my other self, when it let its mask drop. And a deep-down suspicion that I don't know anything for sure about who I used to be.'

Penny thought about that for a while.

'Would you even be able to talk to the AI?' she said finally. 'You could barely communicate with the computer we found under Harrow House. You recognized it as your people's technology, but the AI was so alien that just hearing its voice was enough to freak us out.'

'That computer dated back to Victorian times,' I said. 'If my people have been coming here for centuries, they should have picked up the local language by now.'

Penny nodded, fixing me with her intent gaze. 'What else do you remember from that first day?'

'The stars seemed very bright – like so many unblinking eyes, watching me from on high. I wanted to run away and hide from them. I remember stumbling through narrow streets. The flat yellow light from the street lamps, and parked cars like sleeping sentries . . . There was no one else around, and no lights on in any of the houses I passed.'

'So no one saw you?'

'As far as I know.'

'Why didn't you knock on someone's door and ask for help?'

'The information in my head suggested that would be a very bad idea,' I said. 'Small towns don't care much for strangers, and no one was stranger than me. So I just kept going, all the way through the town and out the other side, until finally I came to a main road and was picked up by a passing car.'

'That was lucky,' said Penny.

'I've often thought that,' I said. 'The odds of someone turning up at such an early hour in the morning, just when I needed someone . . . But thank God for him. He was happy to talk, and I was happy to listen, and by the time he finally dropped me off in the next city, I thought I'd picked up enough to pass for human.'

'What were you wearing?' Penny said suddenly. 'I mean, if you'd only just been made human, where did your clothes come from?'

'The same place as this body,' I said.

'Oh, ick,' said Penny. 'But you're missing the point. I think that you were always supposed to be human; that the ship was ready to make the change, because its crew had work to do here. As humans.'

I nodded slowly. 'Perhaps we were shot down because we were coming here.'

'To Earth?'

'Or maybe to Norton Hedley.'

'What happened next?' said Penny.

'I made my way to London, where Department Y took me under its wing. They had a gift for picking up strays with useful talents. The Department gave me a place to be and useful work to do, while I learned what it meant to be human. It helped that this was the sixties; there were a lot of strange people about, back then. I fitted right in.'

'You haven't talked much about this other survivor,' said Penny. 'I thought you'd be happier now you weren't the only one like you.'

'Knowing he exists just raises a whole new set of questions,' I said. 'Why didn't I remember him until Mr Nemo dug him out of my head? Why has he spent his whole life in one small country town? And, most importantly, is he human like me or has he given in to his alien side?'

'Why do you always have to go for the worst-case scenario?' said Penny.

'Bitter experience,' I said.

'Have you any idea how you could have possibly forgotten something as important as this?'

'Perhaps I was made to forget.'

'By the transformation machines?' said Penny.

'Or by whoever programmed them. In which case, were my memories suppressed out of malice or to protect me? It's always possible there were reasons why I couldn't be allowed to remember anything – alien considerations that my human self could never hope to understand.'

'If we follow that path, we'll never get anywhere,' Penny said briskly. 'We have to assume there are useful answers to be found.'

I looked at her thoughtfully.

'What?' she said.

'How would you feel,' I said carefully, 'if I asked you to stay here, while I went to Norton Hedley on my own?'

Penny smiled at me sweetly. 'Do you think you're about to say something that dumb?'

'It could be dangerous.'

'Which of our cases hasn't been dangerous? Think of all the bad people and weird monsters we've faced! I've proved I can look after myself. Besides, you need me to keep you focused and watch your back.'

'But . . .'

'I am going, Ishmael,' Penny said sternly.

'Of course you are,' I said.

The doorbell rang, and Penny went to answer it. I took a deep breath as I got to my feet, bracing myself for whatever the finished report might bring. Penny came back in from the hall.

'Guess who's come to see us, darling.'

She stepped to one side, and the Colonel came in and nodded briskly to me. Impeccably tailored as always, in a Savile Row suit and his old school tie, the Colonel was a tall, assured sort in his early forties. Handsome enough, in a supercilious sort of way, right down to the neatly trimmed military moustache, and so stiff-backed you could use him as an ironing board. He was carrying a briefcase. I tried not to stare at it.

'Colonel,' I said, 'I wasn't expecting you to deliver the report in person. Don't you have people to do that kind of thing for you?'

'I am supposed to be your only contact point with the Organization,' he said dryly. 'Even if this is not, strictly speaking, Organization business.'

He looked around Penny's flat and tried hard not to wince.

He'd never visited us before, and I think the sheer variety of colours was new to him.

'Sit down, Colonel, and have a nice cup of tea,' Penny said sweetly. 'It's good for culture shock.'

'I'm not staying,' he said quickly.

'Sit down,' I said. 'I just know I'm going to have a whole bunch of questions about what you've brought me, so plant yourself and take the weight off. You're among friends. Sort of.'

Penny smiled remorselessly at the Colonel until he lowered himself stiffly into a chair with a zebra-hide pattern, still clinging firmly to his briefcase. He didn't look at all comfortable, either because of what was in the report or because he didn't approve of discussing secret business in a domestic setting. Penny and I settled ourselves cosily on the sofa.

'The Organization agreed to help with this particular matter, in return for your helping Mr Whisper over the Harrow House problem,' said the Colonel. 'I am only here to deliver the results of the investigation you requested.'

'Do you know Whisper?' I said.

'I don't talk about the Organization to you,' said the Colonel, 'any more than I talk about you to the Organization.'

'But Mr Whisper is a high-up person inside it?' said Penny.

'That is entirely possible,' said the Colonel.

'Does he run the Organization?' I said.

'Which part of "I don't talk about this" are you having trouble grasping?' the Colonel said sternly.

'There must be something you can tell us,' said Penny.

'Mr Whisper does not run the Organization,' the Colonel said carefully. 'But when he speaks, people listen – and not just inside the Organization.'

Penny looked at me. 'I'm no wiser.'

'That's security for you,' I said. 'Please thank Whisper, Colonel, for setting up the investigation.'

The Colonel looked at me steadily. 'It might not be wise to get too close to him.'

'Why not?' said Penny.

'Because it's never a good idea to get close to people who

give you orders,' said the Colonel. 'No matter how friendly you may think you are, if the time comes when a superior has to declare you expendable, he will – and without a moment's hesitation.'

'Is that why you always keep a distance from us?' said Penny. 'Even after we helped you out in the Case of the Missing Mummy?'

'Ours is a professional relationship,' said the Colonel. 'And best left that way.'

'If you had an opinion about Whisper,' I said, 'what do you suppose it might be?'

The Colonel sighed quietly as he realized I wasn't about to let this go.

'It's not my business to have an opinion,' he said. 'If you question the man, you might start to doubt his orders, and that's how the chain of command breaks down.'

'So you never question anything you're told to do?' I said.

'I don't have that luxury,' said the Colonel. 'Which is why, should you decide to follow up anything in the report, I would suggest you do it on your own, without the Organization's support.'

'Because if I do it with their help, they'll want to tell me how to do it,' I said.

'Got it in one,' said the Colonel. 'And they would almost certainly insist on being party to everything you discovered. You might not want that.'

He unsnapped his briefcase, brought out a large file and dumped it on the nearest side table with a heavy thump. I had to raise an eyebrow; I hadn't realized there was that much of interest to be found in Norton Hedley.

'I'm only looking for one man,' I said.

'You wanted to know everything there was to know – about the man, the town and all the weird and unusual occurrences connected to them,' said the Colonel.

'How many pages are there in that thing?' said Penny, eyeing the file as if it might bite.

'Hundreds,' said the Colonel, and then he paused to consider his next words carefully. 'The investigation turned out to be rather more extensive than anticipated. Because of the sheer amount of material involved, we found it necessary to reach out to another group to help us get it done.'

Penny and I looked at each other. Something in the Colonel's voice suggested we should ask the obvious question but that we weren't going to like the answer.

'Which other group?' said Penny.

'Black Heir,' said the Colonel.

I hit him with my best cold stare. 'You brought them in? You must know they can't be trusted to keep anything to themselves.'

'I am aware you have a history when it comes to Black Heir,' said the Colonel.

'I don't like them even knowing I'm involved in this,' I said.

'Your name was never mentioned,' said the Colonel. 'The Black Heir agents were only told what to look for, not who wanted to know.'

I didn't let up on the cold stare. 'But once they start talking about what they've discovered, all the other underground groups will want to get involved. Norton Hedley will be packed full of secret agents pretending to be tourists.'

'Once you authorized us to express an interest in the town, it was inevitable that other parties would become interested,' said the Colonel.

'Have you read the file?' I said, letting the matter drop. For the moment.

'Just the overview,' said the Colonel. 'It is a very lengthy report, and I am extremely busy.'

'Weren't you curious?' asked Penny.

The Colonel managed a small smile. 'I already have enough on my plate to be curious about.'

'What was the Organization's reaction to the file?' I said. 'And don't tell me they haven't read it.'

'Of course they have,' said the Colonel. 'They paid for it. They were . . . intrigued by the town's extensive weird background, and not a little amazed that they had managed to overlook it for so long. So you'd better get your visit to the town in first, before they decide to send someone official.'

'I can't help noticing that you haven't asked why Ishmael is so interested,' said Penny.

'He doesn't ask about my secrets, and I don't inquire about his.'

Penny raised an elegant eyebrow. 'You have secrets?'

'Of course,' said the Colonel. 'I work for the Organization.'

'What do you think is going on in Norton Hedley?' I asked bluntly.

He just shrugged, apparently entirely uninterested. Of course, with the Colonel, you could never be sure.

'Somewhere has to be the strangest place in England. It's probably just a statistical anomaly.'

I looked at the huge file. 'And this is all the available information?'

'The entire weird history of Norton Hedley,' said the Colonel. 'Some of it going back centuries. So read, digest and draw your own conclusions.'

'I was thinking I might take a little holiday down that way,' I said. 'I hear there's some very pretty countryside.'

The Colonel nodded. 'Try not to take too long. There is always the chance we might have need of your particular talents, to do some real work.'

He snapped his briefcase shut and got to his feet, looking a little relieved now the whole social interaction thing was over. Penny and I got to our feet, both of us a little surprised that the Colonel wasn't already heading straight for the door. He gave me a thoughtful look.

'I hope you find what you're looking for, Mr Jones. They say closure can have many benefits.'

Just when you think you've got the man fathomed, he surprises you by doing something human. I nodded my thanks, but he'd already turned away. Penny escorted him out, while I stood and stared at the file on the side table. Then Penny came back, and we both looked at it.

'That is a big file,' said Penny.

'Very big,' I said.

'Bigger than you expected?'

'Oh, yes.'

Penny sighed. 'This is going to take a while. Do you want to split it in two?'

'No,' I said. 'I need to know everything, and I want to hear your opinion on everything.'

'Then I'd better make us some coffee,' said Penny. She headed for the kitchen. 'Don't feel like you have to help.'

I went after her. Because that's all part of living together.

We sat down together with the file before us. Penny looked at me.

'Why are you so interested in all this weird stuff? I thought this was all about finding the other crash survivor?'

'You remember the alien we met during the Case of the Missing Mummy?' I said carefully. 'It said that its people and mine have been at war for longer than our recorded histories. That generations of its kind and mine have died with their teeth buried in each other's throats.'

'Of course I remember,' said Penny. 'But what's that got to do with Norton Hedley?'

'I don't believe my ship crashed where it did by accident. I think the town matters. That it's important to me. And that there's more to me than meets the eye.'

'I had noticed,' Penny said dryly.

I looked at her steadily.

'Back when we were investigating the Hole in Brass-knocker Hill, one of my own kind came looking for me. He wanted to take me back where we came from. He told me I held a high position there, with duties and responsibilities. But going with him would have meant leaving you behind, since you couldn't survive where we'd be going. So I told him I had no intention of going back.'

Penny stared at me. 'Why didn't you tell me this before?'

'I'm telling you now. I don't want there to be any secrets between us, now we're getting ready to uncover the secrets of my past.'

Penny suddenly smiled dazzlingly. 'Maybe you're an alien prince!'

'Maybe,' I said kindly.

'Oh, sweetie – what you gave up, for me . . .'

'I didn't want it,' I said.

'You might not, but what about the other you?'

'It didn't say a word.'

We turned to the file, set out on the table before us like an unexploded bomb.

'Why don't we just skip straight to the index and see if there's anything about a crashed alien ship?' said Penny.

'Because that's not what we're looking for,' I said patiently. 'I want to know what effect the crash had on the town and its people. And if there's any obvious reason why the other survivor chose to live there.'

We worked our way through the file, page by page, all through the evening and on into the early hours.

Norton Hedley was a very old town. It hadn't grown out of any natural gathering place; people just suddenly came together in the sixth century and built it. For no reason that was ever made clear. After that, it never grew much or achieved anything of importance. Norton Hedley was just a small country town, and apparently happy to stay that way.

The only strange thing about the town was its really weird history.

The file listed odd and unexplained events going back centuries. Which was, to be fair, not that unusual where small country towns are concerned. England's history is built on layers of the strange and uncanny. Sometimes openly, sometimes not . . . but it's always there. After a while, I did skip ahead, just to see how much more of this stuff we had to get through, and was astonished to discover it made up most of the file.

'Did you know about this?' said Penny.

'No,' I said. 'And I should have. A town with this much weird stuff attached to it should have set off alarms in all the underground groups I worked for.'

'Maybe the town just likes to keep itself to itself,' said Penny.

'My ship crashed in a field right outside Weird Shit Central,' I said. 'That can't be a coincidence.'

Penny frowned. 'But what does an alien starship have to do with all these weird happenings?'

'Good question,' I said. 'Keep reading.'

There were a lot of strange sightings in and around Norton Hedley. Unusual beasts that came and went, leaving tracks that couldn't be identified and deep claw marks gouged into people's doors. Ghosts of every kind – from dim figures that walked through walls, to dead voices on the telephone, to repeated visions of an old manor house that had burned down centuries before. There were also a great many unexplained disappearances, from the distant past right up to the present day. Far too many for one small country town. I checked the dates, but there was no obvious rise in numbers after the ship crashed.

'Most of this is just traditional weird stuff,' I said. 'But this many people going missing? It's almost as if something is taking a tithe from the town.'

'You think something happened to make all these people vanish without a trace?' said Penny.

'Something or someone,' I said. 'All those people can't just have been murdered, because no one ever found any bodies.'

'They could have simply upped and left,' said Penny. 'People are always turning their backs on small towns and disappearing over the next horizon, lured away by the bright lights of the big city.'

'Then why did none of them ever contact their families afterwards?' I said.

Penny frowned. 'Ishmael . . . how can we be sure all this weird stuff isn't simply a distraction, to keep us from noticing what's really important?'

'We can't,' I said. 'Keep reading.'

There were all kinds of stories. Footsteps heard walking past houses in the early hours of the morning, but on the few occasions when people felt brave enough to look out of their windows, there was never anybody there. Scarecrows who kept changing their positions at night until they were moved to a different field. Skulls that refused to stay decently buried and returned to their old homes by unknown ways, screaming horribly if anyone tried to take them out to bury them again. Streets that weren't always there; a wood where people saw disturbing things; unknown creatures that would come right up to the edge of town, but never enter. Lights in the sky, and voices in the night.

Penny and I looked at each other after that last one, remembering the computer we found under Harrow House, which had tried to reach out to people but only succeeded in terrifying them because its voice was so utterly alien.

'Could the voices they're hearing be coming from your ship's AI?' asked Penny. 'Trying to tell someone where it is?'

'It shouldn't want anyone to know,' I said. 'That's why the ship buried itself in the first place.'

Finally, we came to the incident I was looking for. In 1963, half the people in Norton Hedley stood outside in their streets and watched a falling star streak across the night sky. Most of them thought it was just a meteor, but no impact site was ever found. Several books mentioned it as a possible UFO, but even though a lot of people spent a lot of time looking for a landing site, no one ever turned up any evidence. Of course, that's never been enough to stop people believing what they want to believe.

'This report isn't what you were expecting, is it?' said Penny.

'I'm not sure what I expected,' I said. 'But this definitely isn't it. We're going to have to visit Norton Hedley and work out what's going on for ourselves.'

'Of course,' said Penny. 'That's what we do.'

We kept on reading, until at last the report's authors were ready to identify the man they thought I was looking for. A local author, Vincent Smith, had been researching the town folklore for decades and had written a number of books on the subject, one of them about the possible UFO. Apparently, he'd spent years trying to dig up evidence on it. Which was enough for the file's authors to declare him a Person of Interest.

'Does the name ring a bell?' said Penny.

I frowned and shook my head. Penny fired up her laptop and searched for Vincent Smith's bibliography. There were a lot of books listed, all of them concerned with the town's weird history. Penny found a cover photo, and my heart missed a beat.

'That's him!' I said, leaning in for a closer look. 'That's

the face I saw when Mr Nemo unlocked the old memories in my head.'

'Smith and Jones,' said Penny. 'I should have known. But if you knew what he looked like, why didn't you give the investigating team a description?'

'Because I had no memory at all of that face . . . until I just saw it,' I said.

'OK,' said Penny. 'That's a bit weird, isn't it?'

'You have no idea,' I said.

Smith's books had pretty basic titles: *Local Ley Lines*, *The Wandering Scarecrows*, *Voices in the Dark*. And not one of them had ever come close to troubling the bestseller lists.

'Do you want to press on and get through the rest of the file?' said Penny. 'There's still some way to go.'

'It can wait,' I said. 'This is what I was looking for.'

Penny found some more photos. Smith as a young man, then middle-aged, and finally a distinguished grey-haired gentleman in his eighties.

'How can he be the other crash survivor when he's aged so much?' said Penny.

'Perhaps the transformation machines weren't able to do as good a job on him as they did on me,' I said. 'He might have no idea he's anything more than human. The first evidence I had was that I wasn't aging.'

'And that your blood is golden,' said Penny.

'Yes,' I said. 'He couldn't have overlooked that. Unless the transformation machines made him more human than me.'

'If the machines made you human so you could fit in,' Penny said slowly, 'why did they give you golden blood and keep you from aging?'

'I always assumed there were some aspects of me they couldn't change and still preserve my hidden self.' I studied Smith's most recent photo. 'He looks the age I should be now.'

'We need to be sure this is the right man before we talk to him,' said Penny. 'We don't want his next book to be all about this mysterious stranger who came into his life and started asking all kinds of weird questions.'

'I have to talk to him,' I said. 'The machines stole my past and left me vulnerable to my enemies, and I'm starting to wonder whether that might have been deliberate. If they were instructed to do that by the ship's AI . . . or because Smith made them do it.'

Penny looked at me sharply. 'Why would he want to?'

'So I wouldn't know he existed.'

Penny looked as if she wanted to say *Why?* again, but she didn't.

'Do you still want to talk to someone who'd do that?'

'More than ever,' I said. 'This man could have answers to all the questions of my life.'

'I thought you didn't care about your alien past,' Penny said carefully. 'That you were determined to stay human.'

'I am,' I said. 'But I need to know what it is I'm turning my back on. If only so it can't sneak up on me. And on top of that . . . I have to assume my ancient enemies are still out there looking for me.'

Penny shuddered briefly. 'I really don't like the idea of aliens moving among us, unseen and unsuspected . . .'

'Another good reason to talk to Vincent Smith,' I said. 'To warn him that he has enemies. Who might or might not be human.'

Penny consulted her laptop. 'There's an address for him, but no Facebook, phone number or e-mail. Which is a bit odd, for a writer. He should at least have his own website, so he could publicize his books.'

'Someone who limits and controls his contacts with the outside world,' I said. 'That fits.'

'Assuming he really is who you want him to be,' said Penny, 'what would you say to him?'

I smiled. 'Where have you been all my life?'

Penny shook her head. 'Oh, this can only go well.'

TWO

And Black Heir Makes Three

T
he good thing about long train journeys is that they give you plenty of time to think. And I had a lot to think about.

It took Penny and me three different trains to get from London to Norton Hedley, deep in the heart of the South-West countryside. Where myth and legend have always walked hand in hand with history, even when they weren't talking to each other. I spent most of the journey staring out of the window and scowling to myself. Penny could tell I needed to be alone with my thoughts, so she immersed herself in the latest issue of the *Fortean Times*. Preparing herself for all the weird stuff waiting in Norton Hedley.

The nearer we drew to the town, the darker my thoughts became. Mile by mile, I was getting closer to the point where I would finally be in a position to unearth the true facts behind my beginnings, and I had to wonder if that was what my previous self had been waiting for, all these years; if the truth, whatever it turned out to be, would be the key in the lock to let Mr Hyde out at last. I'd always suspected I was just the mask on the face of the monster, the human dream of the sleeping alien . . .

What would happen to me when my original self no longer needed me? What happens to a dream when the dreamer wakes and remembers who they really are? Questions without answers until we got to Norton Hedley.

For a long time, Penny and I were the only passengers in our carriage, and I couldn't help but notice that while people left the train at various stations along the way, no one seemed to be getting on to replace them. The train was emptying out as we drew nearer Norton Hedley, and I was starting to wonder if everyone else knew something Penny and I didn't.

As we started our final approach to the town, I studied the countryside carefully, to see if it would let its disguise slip and show me a glimpse of the real face underneath. So I could look it in the eye and stare it down. The scenery seemed pleasant enough, with wide open fields under a cloudless blue sky, low stone walls and neatly trimmed hedges, and sheep and horses standing around like window dressing. The only ominous prospect was provided by rows of leafless trees standing guard on the horizon. Dark slender shapes like letters in some ancient alphabet, spelling out a warning in a language no one understood any more.

The more I looked at the countryside, the more it seemed as if something was looking back. Perhaps the town itself, wondering why I was coming home after so long away. And preparing a very special welcome for its prodigal son.

Penny became aware that something had caught my attention. She took a quick look out of the window and then closed her magazine and leaned forward.

'Ishmael? What's wrong? You look like someone just dug up your coffin and knocked on the lid.'

I deliberately turned my gaze away from the countryside and managed a smile for her.

'It feels like someone up ahead knows we're coming – and not in a good way.'

Penny just nodded. She trusted my instincts in these matters.

'Any idea who it might be?'

I wanted to say *Not who – what*, but I wasn't ready to go that far.

'Most of the subterranean groups have spent years chasing rumours of my existence,' I said. 'And, of course, there's always the enemy aliens, and their human agents.'

Penny met my gaze squarely, and I knew I hadn't fooled her.

'You've always known about them,' she said. 'And never given anything even resembling a damn. You usually look forward to walking into a trap, because it means a chance to kick someone's arse. So what's different this time? What's put that wary look in your eyes?'

'I don't know,' I said, trying hard not to frown. 'I just have this feeling . . . that I'm heading into a situation I don't understand, to face something so off the chart I can't even put a name to it.'

'Could it be the ship's AI reaching out to you?'

'No,' I said. 'When I finally make contact with my old ship, I think that will feel like coming home. What I can feel waiting is completely outside of my experience. And I've been around.'

Penny looked out of the carriage window. 'I can see the station. We're almost there.'

'I should have brought a gun,' I said. 'A really big gun. With big glowing thermonuclear bullets.'

'Stop that,' Penny said briskly. 'That's not you.'

You don't really know me, I thought. *And I'm not sure that I do.*

We finally disembarked at a small, old-fashioned station. The kind of setting where all the more picturesque elements have been carefully preserved in aspic, to please the tourists. No one else got off the train. Penny and I stood close together, the only people on an empty platform, ready to face whatever came our way.

The blunt utilitarian station house looked like it pre-dated Beeching and his cuts. All the windows were covered by rough wooden shutters, and the only signs of life came from an overabundance of fresh flowers, set out on display to try to make the place seem more cheerful and welcoming. I couldn't say it was working. There could have been a brass band playing, and the town mayor presenting me with a really big key and the freedom of the town, and I would still have felt as if I had just walked into an ambush.

'I hate to be the one to rain on your spooky feeling,' said Penny, 'but I'm not seeing anything even remotely threatening. In fact, I'm not seeing anything at all.'

'You say that like it's a good thing,' I said. 'Where is everyone?'

'Norton Hedley is a small country town,' she said patiently. 'And we are way out of the tourist season. The locals are probably sitting at home, looking at all the cheap tat they couldn't shift and waiting for summer to come round again.'

'Then why do I feel like I'm staring down the barrel of a gun?'

'We could just get back on the train,' said Penny. 'Wrong-foot the bastards, and come back some other time.'

'No,' I said. 'The more this town tries to intimidate me, to stop me from getting to the truth, the more it proves how important that must be.'

'Well,' said Penny, 'that didn't sound at all paranoid.'

'Oh, good,' I said. 'Because I wasn't sure.'

The train pulled out of the station as though determined to put Norton Hedley behind it as quickly as possible, leaving Penny and me standing alone on the platform. In the heavy quiet that followed the train's departure, I suddenly felt very conspicuous – as though I'd finally stepped out from behind the cover of my life and revealed myself to unseen watching eyes. I looked up and down the empty platform, but nothing looked back.

Penny shot me a bright smile, slipped her arm through mine and squeezed it comfortingly against her side.

'You were so quiet all the way here, I assume you've been putting together a plan of action. Something we could start doing right now?'

'Well, first, we locate Vincent Smith and ask him a whole bunch of questions,' I said.

'Yes, I got that,' Penny said patiently. 'But we didn't come all this way just to talk to one man. What if he isn't the other crash survivor, or doesn't remember anything, like you? What do we do then? Hire a mechanical digger and excavate every field bordering Norton Hedley until we find your ship? Or just roll up our sleeves and interrogate everyone in town?'

'I will if I have to,' I said. 'Someone here knows what I need to know, and I am ready to pick this whole town up and shake it until the one person who knows the truth falls out.'

'But what if this town isn't what you think it is?' said Penny.

I looked at her sharply. 'How do you mean?'

'What if Norton Hedley isn't anything like the image you

have in your head from reading about it in the report? What if its secrets and mysteries are actually nothing to do with you and your ship?'

'No,' I said. 'There's something here. I can feel it. For once, everything really is all about me.'

'Fine,' said Penny. 'But where do we start?'

'The Pale Horse Hotel,' I said. 'I booked us a room. There's bound to be a bar, and people always like to talk in a hotel bar.'

Penny nodded quickly, relieved that at least now we had a starting point.

'And then we go and talk to Vincent Smith?'

No, I thought. *I don't think I'm ready, just yet, to confront the one man who might know the true meaning and purpose of my life.*

'Let's get a feel for the town first,' I said. 'Talk to people, dig into Smith's background a little.'

'What if he hears we're asking questions about him and makes a run for it?' said Penny.

'Then we'll know he's worth chasing,' I said. 'But I think there's more to this than just him. There's something about this town . . .'

'You haven't even seen it yet,' said Penny.

'Then why do I feel like we're being watched by someone with really big eyes and even bigger teeth?'

'A lifetime working as a secret agent?' Penny said sweetly.

'Just because I'm paranoid doesn't mean I'm not out to get you,' I said solemnly.

And then we were both caught by surprise, as an almost aggressively cheerful young woman burst out of the station house and came striding down the platform towards us, waving her arm urgently, just in case we might have missed her.

'Hello, hello, Ishmael Jones and Penny Belcourt! Welcome to Norton Hedley! I'm Lucy Parker, assigned to provide you with all possible support and assistance!'

She crashed to a halt before us, beaming all over her face and looking very pleased with herself. I fixed her with a stern look, but it did nothing to curb her enthusiasm. Lucy Parker was an attractive, sharp-faced blonde in her mid-twenties, barely five feet tall and dressed in a smart white linen suit, complete with a black carnation in her buttonhole.

'I work for Black Heir,' she said cheerfully. 'But that doesn't necessarily mean I'm a bad person. So! Just tell me what you need and it's all yours, Mr Jones.'

'To start with, keep your voice down,' I said. 'And a little less of the names in public. There's no need to advertise our presence.'

'What public?' said Lucy, gesturing expansively at the deserted platform. 'Anyway, it's not like Ishmael Jones is your real name. Everyone knows that.'

'It's still a well-known name in certain circles,' I said.

'I know!' said Lucy. 'Will you please unclench? I got here early just so I could check out the station for suspicious types, and there is definitely no one else within shooting distance.'

'Do you know where everyone is?' said Penny.

'You picked the wrong time of year to visit Norton Hedley, if you didn't want to stand out,' said Lucy. 'It's well past summer, and once there's no one left to sell dubious souvenirs to, the locals prefer to keep themselves to themselves. The streets are so empty you could kick a pig up and down them and no one would notice. If you ask me, at this time of year they should just rename the town Marie Celeste and get it over with. Is there anything more depressing than a tourist trap when there's no one around for the locals to put on a pleasant face for? Like a night club in the daylight, with all its makeup rubbed off.'

I put up a hand to stop the verbal assault. Lucy broke off and looked at me expectantly.

'Why are you here?' I said bluntly.

'Black Heir sent me to assist you, as a courtesy to the Organization. Because my superiors owe your superiors a favour.'

'What kind of favour?' I said.

Lucy shrugged. 'They didn't tell me.'

'Would you tell me if they had?' I asked.

'Almost certainly not,' Lucy said happily. 'You have your secrets, and we have ours. But since we were brought in to help run your original investigation, Black Heir will, of course, be very interested in anything you might happen to discover here and wish to share with us.'

I smiled inwardly, feeling a little easier now I'd caught Lucy in her first lie. The Colonel had been very clear that my name was never mentioned. Although if Black Heir had wanted to find out why the Organization was so keen to turn over all the stones in one out-of-the-way country town, it wouldn't have been that difficult for a group with their resources to make an educated guess.

'Why is Black Heir so ready to help?' said Penny, since I was still standing there, saying nothing, as I worked my way through my thoughts.

'Because of the meteor that never landed,' said Lucy. 'That particular account did stand out just a bit, compared with all the general weird stuff. And crashed alien ships are very definitely Black Heir's remit.' She didn't even try not to sound possessive about that, as she looked at me hopefully. 'Is that why you've come here, Mr Jones?'

'I'm looking for someone,' I said. 'And I don't need any assistance from Black Heir.'

Lucy kept on smiling, determined to be pleasant and accommodating if it killed her. 'But there are all kinds of things I can do for you, Mr Jones – many of them entirely legal. I can provide local knowledge, introduce you to all the right people and supply legwork as required.'

'Why did Black Heir choose you as their representative?' asked Penny.

Lucy shrugged cheerfully. 'I volunteered. Working with two renowned field agents like you could make my career if we turn up something worth finding.'

'And if I were to tell you to go back to Black Heir and leave us alone?' I said.

Lucy shrugged again. 'They'd only send someone else to dog your every step. Bringing Black Heir into your investigation couldn't help but get the higher-ups interested, and now they won't let go until they know what's going on. Your people must have realized that would happen when they made the decision to involve us.'

Yes, I thought. *So why did they do it? What's really going on here, that no one is telling me?*

Lucy kept on chattering, apparently not even a little unnerved by the way I was staring steadily at her and saying nothing. Because I knew better than most never to trust anyone from Black Heir.

It hadn't escaped my notice that Lucy was giving me most of her attention, and barely even glancing at Penny; doing her best to come across as a star-struck fan, eager for any pearl of wisdom that might happen to drop from my lips. I was a little concerned Penny might be jealous, but a quick glance in her direction assured me she was simply amused by the situation. She could tell I wasn't buying any of Lucy's performance, and was waiting to see when the penny would drop for Lucy. Who just kept chattering on.

'At least with me, you know where you are! You can keep an eye on me, tell me as much or as little as you like, steer me away from anything you don't want me looking at too closely. I don't mind. Honestly.'

I used to work for Black Heir, back in the 1980s, under another name and identity. Until I had to disappear abruptly, when they started taking too close an interest in my background. The current administration shouldn't have any idea I was that person, but I've never been sure how much Black Heir knows about anything. I considered Lucy thoughtfully as she stood beaming brightly in front of me, and then glanced at Penny, who was too busy being amused to provide any support.

Penny had no idea just how dangerous Black Heir could be. She thought they were all about information gathering and making use of salvaged alien technology. But I knew that in any given situation, you could always rely on Black Heir to do whatever was in their best interests, and to hell with everyone else. Black Heir field agents could eat Men in Black for breakfast.

'The Organization never mentioned anything to us about being met by a Black Heir field agent,' I said finally.

Lucy nodded quickly. 'I'm told it was only agreed at the last moment, while you were still travelling here. I'm surprised your people haven't contacted you. Do you want to phone home and ask?'

Normally, that would have been correct procedure, but this wasn't an official Organization operation. Black Heir should have known that. Or perhaps they did, and had used the ambiguity of the situation to muscle their way in. It was the kind of thing they did. Even so, the Organization wouldn't have just thrown me to the wolves . . . Unless there really was something else going on.

Penny stirred at my side, a little uncomfortable that I was still standing there saying nothing. She cleared her throat, and Lucy immediately switched her big beaming smile to her.

'What makes you the right person for this job, Lucy?' said Penny. Just to be saying something.

'Oh, I'm local,' said Lucy. 'I grew up just a few towns over.'

'Have you been told why we're here?' Penny asked.

'Only that you're interested in the local weird stuff,' said Lucy. 'And I know all there is to know about that. You can't grow up around here without being force-fed all that nonsense from a very early age. You can't image how much of a shock it was, when I joined Black Heir and discovered some of this stuff was real. I was made part of the original research team because I knew all the right directions to point people in.'

'Have you ever seen anything weird around here?' said Penny.

'No! Not a thing!' said Lucy. 'I'm not even a proper field agent. This is my first actual assignment. But now I'm working with the notorious Ishmael Jones and Penny Belcourt, I expect to be hip-deep in weird stuff by nightfall!'

'You've heard of us?' said Penny.

'Of course!' said Lucy. 'Your reputation precedes you, waving a big red flag and yelling for everyone else to get out of the way. If you're interested in this town, that means there must be something here worth being interested in, and I can't wait to find out what it is. Mind you, Norton Hedley is more than a bit freaky, on the quiet. The only reason it isn't a fixture on the weird happenings map is because the town council has always gone to great pains to cover up the more unpleasant stuff, so as not to scare off the tourists. Spooky stories and weird folklore bring them in, but genuinely strange stuff and bad happenings lead to traumatized accounts on Tripadvisor and no summer money next year . . . Do you really need me to clue you in on this stuff? It's all in the report.'

'Have you read it?' I said.

Lucy frowned. 'Only the bits I worked on. Life's too short to wade through that many rural legends.'

I looked at her thoughtfully. 'What did Black Heir know about Norton Hedley before the Organization brought you into the investigation?'

'They'd never even heard of the place,' Lucy said immediately. 'The higher-ups were astonished by the sheer amount of weird stories we uncovered. But I can tell you for a fact that most of these supposed ancient myths and legends were actually created by the townspeople to attract and entertain tourists. In the off-season, people around here get together in bars of an evening, just to come up with new traditional stories for the next season.'

'Does that include the UFO in the sixties?' I said, as casually as I could.

'No, that one seems solid enough,' she said. 'People really did see a meteor, and there was a lot of talk about a possible UFO landing, but there's never been any evidence to support it. Or Black Heir would have been all over the town, long before this.'

'Do you believe in the weird stuff, now you're part of Black Heir?' asked Penny.

'I suppose they can't all be made-up stories,' said Lucy. 'But how do you sort the wheat from the chaff, without any proof? When it comes to the older stories, there aren't even any witnesses left alive to talk to.'

'Speaking of people who aren't around any more,' I said, 'what can you tell us about the large number of people who've gone missing from the town?'

Lucy nodded quickly. 'You might have something there. I'd heard about it, of course, but I was shocked when I saw the real numbers. If I lived in a town like this, I'd move. And keep on moving till I couldn't even see the town any more, before whatever it is that's happening decided to happen to me.'

She broke off and looked expectantly at me and Penny . . . until it became clear we weren't going to say anything, and then she just shrugged again and hit us with her brightest smile.

'Don't worry; it was made very clear to me that you're in charge. I'm only here to provide assistance. So! Where do you want to go first?'

'We're booked into the Pale Horse,' I said.

Lucy grimaced. 'I'd tell you to go somewhere else, but unfortunately there isn't anywhere else. The Pale Horse is famously a bit of a dump. Far too concerned with appearing charming and olde-worldly, instead of investing in modern comforts. And don't trust anything that comes out of their kitchen, unless your stomach is used to roughing it. Where's your luggage?'

'We didn't plan on staying long,' I said.

'Bound to attract attention, turning up at a hotel with no luggage,' said Lucy. 'Still! We can always say it's on its way. OK, follow me. There aren't any taxis, so we'll have to step it out. But Norton Hedley is such a small town that nowhere is ever very far from anywhere else.'

'Don't you have a car?' said Penny.

'I had to leave it parked on the other side of town,' said Lucy.

She started towards the station house, but I refused to be hurried. I stood my ground, so Penny did too, and Lucy had no choice but to turn around and come back.

If you knew you were meeting us at the station, why didn't you drive your car here? I thought. And then I smiled inwardly. *Because this way you can take us through the town at your own speed, and hope that will give you enough time to charm us into spilling some useful information.*

'How did the original investigation go?' I asked. 'Were the local people cooperative?'

'Oh, they couldn't do enough to help,' said Lucy. 'They're always up for a chance to show off and tell their stories to visitors. But the moment we started pressing them for a few actual facts, some of them did turn a bit surly. Still! Nothing we couldn't cope with.'

'Tell me you didn't antagonize the townspeople,' I said sternly.

'Of course not,' said Lucy. 'Why would you even ask?'

'Because you're Black Heir,' I said.

'This way!' said Lucy, gesturing determinedly at the station house. 'Lots to see, lots of places to go! You know, I couldn't believe it when they told me you'd be arriving by train. Such a touristy thing to do.'

She set off again, and this time Penny and I deigned to follow her. I shot a look at Penny that said, *Does she ever shut up?* And Penny looked back: *Beats me.*

Once we'd passed through the station house, which held nothing but shadows and cobwebs, and absolutely no sign it had ever been blessed with actual staff, we found ourselves out in the open and facing the town. Long narrow streets packed full of old-fashioned houses, constructed from creamy local stone and topped with grey slate roofs. It all seemed very calm and peaceful, quaint and picturesque . . . With no sense at all of anything looking back at me.

'Welcome to Norton Hedley!' said Lucy. 'Don't expect too much. This town has weird shit like a dog has fleas, but you could live here all your life and never see anything out of the ordinary. Tons of tourists pass through every summer, and the most exciting thing they ever encounter is the cream tea.'

'Are you always this talkative?' asked Penny. She sounded honestly interested.

'Sorry,' said Lucy. 'Being around two underground legends makes me nervous.'

Penny shot me a look. '*Two* legends . . .'

'You earned it,' I said generously.

'So, what do you think?' said Lucy. 'Is Norton Hedley everything you thought it would be?'

'Not really,' I said. 'Everything's so . . . normal.'

'Told you,' said Lucy. 'All that weird stuff is just stories. Trust me; I've been in and out of this dump, visiting friends, my whole life.'

'So you're not armed?' I said.

'Well, of course I'm armed,' said Lucy. 'I'm Black Heir. Why do you ask?'

'Just a feeling,' I said.

'And you should always respect the feelings of a legendary field agent like Ishmael,' Penny said smoothly.

'I could put in a request to my superiors,' said Lucy. 'Ask for reinforcements. Of course, they'd want to know why.'

'I don't think any amount of armed men would make much difference,' I said.

'OK,' said Lucy. 'Starting to feel seriously spooked now . . .'

'Good,' I said. 'It might keep you alive.'

Lucy smiled determinedly and plunged into the maze of narrow streets like a native guide on safari, alert for any sense of danger, or anything worth pointing at. Penny and I wandered along behind her, taking our time. It all seemed pleasant enough: ivy-covered cottages, rose gardens, Tudor frontages and lozenged windows, and even a few bricked-up windows on the larger buildings, from the days when windows were taxed. The few shops were all tourist traps: small family businesses selling overpriced gifts and tacky mementos, along with tiny tearooms and restaurants with hand-written menus in their windows. Most of them had *Closed* signs, with no indication they had any intention of reopening until there were new tourists to fleece. It was a breath of Olde England, picture postcard perfect . . . And therefore, not quite real. Norton Hedley seemed to me more and more someone's idea of what a small country town ought to be, rather than the real thing. Penny leaned in close.

'Why are you frowning?'

'It feels like this town hasn't changed much in ages. I'm not seeing any modern buildings, or franchises . . . These streets probably looked much the same fifty years ago, or even a hundred.'

It was Penny's turn to frown. 'You think someone preserved the town this way? Why would they want to do that?'

'I don't know,' I said. 'But I keep coming back to my suspicion that the ship didn't crash here by accident. That just possibly it was shot down because it was coming here.'

'Excuse me,' Lucy said respectfully. 'But you're both speaking so quietly I can't make out a word you're saying, even though you obviously understand each other perfectly. How do you do that?'

Penny and I shared a smile. It all came down to years of closeness bordering on telepathy, coupled with my alien nature, but I wasn't about to tell Lucy that.

'Practice,' I said.

'You field agents know all the tricks,' Lucy said admiringly. 'How long have you two been partners? Is it true you once worked a case at Loch Ness? Did you see the monster?'

I tried my stern look again. 'You know we can't talk about any of that.'

'Of course I know,' said Lucy, hitting me with her best disarming smile. 'But I was told to give it a try anyway. The Organization doesn't often let Black Heir in on their operations, so when they reached out to us on this one, it raised eyebrows all the way to the top.'

'This is a personal case,' I said, 'and in no way official Organization business. I'm just here looking for someone.'

'But you must have serious influence inside the Organization to get them to run an investigation this big,' said Lucy. 'And persuade Black Heir to come on board as well.'

'I never asked for that,' I said.

'No one thinks you did,' said Lucy. 'Everyone at Black Heir knows how you feel about them, even if they don't know why. Do you know something about Black Heir, Mr Jones, that us poor working stiffs ought to know?'

I looked at her and said nothing.

Lucy shrugged, entirely unfazed. 'Your business is your business.'

'Why are you so opposed to us staying at the Pale Horse?' I said, not in any way changing the subject.

'Because it's a tourist trap. You wouldn't catch me dead in that overpriced up-itself shit-hole.'

'But didn't you stay there when you were working as part of the investigation team?' said Penny.

Lucy stopped smiling. 'None of us wanted to stay in town

overnight,' she said slowly. 'Not the Organization agents or the Black Heir crew. We all got this feeling, as the evening drew on, that the town could be a very bad place, once night fell. We all got out early and booked into hotels in the surrounding towns.'

'You had a bad feeling about Norton Hedley?' said Penny, glancing at me.

'Like the town didn't want us here,' said Lucy. She took a deep breath, threw off her dark mood and smiled dazzlingly. 'So! Should I take you straight to the appalling hotel, so you can see your room and be disappointed, or do you want me to give you the grand tour first? Because that could take some time . . .'

'I came here to talk to a local author,' I said firmly. 'Vincent Smith. He was identified in the report as the man I might be looking for. Do you know him?'

'No,' said Lucy. She sounded a little surprised I would even think she did.

'I thought he was a local celebrity?' said Penny.

'Whatever gave you that idea?' said Lucy.

'He's written all these books about the local phenomena,' I said.

'Oh, please,' said Lucy. 'There are all kinds of books about Norton Hedley's weird history. Most of them self-published. The weird stuff is pretty much passé, now *The X-Files* isn't a big thing any more. Vincent Smith is a cottage industry, churning out one book after another because none of them ever sell well enough on their own to support him. He was never a big deal – not even in his own town. Perhaps especially not in his own town.'

Lucy broke off and came to a sudden halt. Penny and I stopped with her, and Lucy looked at us uncertainly. For the first time, I thought she looked distinctly unhappy and even a little guilty.

'I was pretty sure you'd want to talk to Smith, so I went straight to his cottage the moment I arrived, yesterday evening. I couldn't get any answer when I knocked on his door, or see anything when I looked through his windows . . . and then a

neighbour came round to hit me with the bad news. I'm sorry
to have to tell you this, but . . . Vincent Smith died yesterday.
Of a heart attack.'

Penny and I looked sharply at each other, and then at Lucy.

'Why didn't you tell us this before?' I said.

'I didn't want to spoil your day with bad news, so soon
after you'd got here,' said Lucy. 'He wasn't an Organization
man, was he? I never came across any evidence that he was
a player.'

'He dies suddenly, the day before we arrive to talk to him?'
said Penny.

'I don't like the sound of that,' I said.

'You think someone got to him?' said Penny. 'To make sure
he couldn't talk to us?'

'There was no question of foul play,' Lucy said immediately.
'Word is, there wasn't a mark on him. He was just a very old
man.'

'Did you talk to him during your investigation?' I asked.
'Did anyone talk to him?'

'Between us, we talked to pretty much everyone,' said Lucy.
'But it was all kept very casual. Smith definitely wasn't
singled out or asked anything the others weren't.'

'Where is he, right now?' I said.

'Lying in state, at the town mortuary,' said Lucy. 'Laid out
on a slab and waiting for his autopsy. Though it could take a
while for anyone to get to him. Towns this small don't tend
to get priority.'

'So no one's disturbed the body yet,' I said. 'Good. Where
is this mortuary?'

'I could take you straight there!' said Lucy. 'If you want.
I know where everywhere is.'

'No,' I said. 'I have something else in mind for you, while
Penny and I go check that Smith really is who we're looking for.'

Lucy grinned delightedly. 'You think the body in the
mortuary might be a ringer? That the real Smith could still
be alive, hiding out somewhere because he doesn't want to
answer questions? Or that someone else could be behind all
this and giving us the old runaround?'

'Wouldn't be the first time,' I said.

'But who would want to do that?' said Lucy. 'What could be so important about one not very successful writer? What could he have to tell you that someone else wouldn't want you to know?'

'You're just full of questions, aren't you?' said Penny.

'That's how you get answers,' she said reasonably.

'Right now, I need you to go to Smith's house and search it thoroughly, for anything out of the ordinary,' I said. 'Make sure you don't miss a thing – and this time, don't let a neighbour see you.'

Lucy bounced up and down on her toes with excitement. 'Proper fieldwork at last! What exactly am I looking for?'

'I think you'll know it when you see it,' I said. 'But whatever you find, you bring it straight to me. I don't want you talking to anyone else about this case, and that very definitely includes your controller at Black Heir. You report only to me. And Penny.'

'Nice save,' said Penny.

I kept my gaze fixed on Lucy. 'If this isn't acceptable, say so now. And we'll agree to go our separate ways.'

Lucy grinned back at me. 'For a chance to work with two legends, it's worth tearing up the rule book. Not that I tend to follow it that much anyway.'

'Good attitude,' said Penny.

'I think so,' said Lucy.

'All right,' I said. 'Go and burgle Vincent Smith's cottage, find something worth finding and then come and look for us. If we're not at the mortuary, try the hotel.'

'Catch you later!' said Lucy.

And off she went, striding determinedly down the street. Penny and I watched her go until we were sure she was safely out of earshot, and then we both relaxed a little.

'Do you think we can trust her?' said Penny.

'Of course not,' I said. 'She's Black Heir. Even if she is what she appears to be, which I doubt.'

'You think all that bright-eyed enthusiasm was a cover?'

'I hope so,' I said. 'I'd hate to think she's really like that.'

'So you sent her off to Smith's cottage to get her out of the way?'

'I don't want her around while we're checking the body,' I said. 'And there is always the possibility she might find something useful at his cottage.'

'And, of course, if anyone's going to get caught burgling a house, better her than us,' said Penny. 'Because we don't have any official protection.'

'Got it in one,' I said.

'What do you think is going on here?' said Penny, gesturing at the town. 'Could Vincent Smith really be dead?'

'Any number of people could have killed him, to stop him talking,' I said. 'But why would they want to? They don't know he's the other crash survivor. No . . . Black Heir field agents aren't known for their subtlety when it comes to asking questions. It's far more likely one of them raised Smith's suspicions enough that he decided to fake his own death.'

'The way you have, in the past,' Penny said evenly. 'When you needed to disappear in a hurry.'

'Of course,' I said. 'No one ever bothers a dead man.'

'But you never left a body behind,' said Penny.

'Which is why we're going to the mortuary,' I said. 'To check the body is still there.'

THREE

The Things You Find in a Mortuary

'You know,' I said, as Penny and I watched Lucy disappear down the street, 'we really ought to have asked her how to find the hospital mortuary before we let her go. Do you think I should call her back?'

Penny sighed. 'Best not to disappoint her faith in two such legendary field agents.' She took out her phone. 'OK . . . I've found the town site, and a map . . . Yes, there's the hospital. It isn't far. Lucy was right: this is a very small town. More like a village, really. Or a hamlet. Do they still have those?'

'I'm not sure what they have here,' I said. 'Let's get to the mortuary before someone else beats us to it.'

Penny looked at me sharply. 'Whom did you have in mind?'

'It's not like there's any shortage of choices,' I said. 'Underground groups, enemy aliens, unknown interested parties and unsuspected weird things. Not forgetting whatever it was I sensed on the train coming in.'

'I don't want to use the word "paranoid" but I'm going to,' said Penny. 'Ishmael, there is no evidence anyone here knows the truth about you or your crashed ship.'

'Vincent Smith is dead,' I said. 'Suddenly and very inconveniently dead. If he didn't fake it, and if he didn't die from natural causes . . .'

'Emphasis on the *if*, in both cases . . .'

'Then that means enemy action. Which is why we should be walking, instead of talking.'

Penny put her phone away and set off down the street. I strolled along beside her, enjoying the quiet afternoon. After a while, Penny shot me a look.

'You are the only person I know who only uses their phone as a phone. One of these days, you're going to have to tiptoe into the twenty-first century and get in step with the rest of us. How can an alien from outer space be such a technophobe?'

'Practice,' I said. 'I have more reason than most to know that tech can turn on you.'

The narrow streets went on and on, surprisingly empty and unnervingly quiet. The roads were entirely free of traffic, and the few people we saw seemed to be going out of their way to keep their distance. I made a point of smiling and nodding politely, but no one responded.

'Why is everyone being so standoffish?' I said quietly to Penny. 'It's almost as though . . .'

'Yes?' said Penny. 'As though what?'

'Beats me,' I said. 'Maybe they're still nursing hurt feelings from the way Black Heir treated their favourite stories. Right now, I'm more concerned with how deserted the streets are. I mean, it's mid-afternoon on a bright sunny day. Where is everyone?'

'Probably watching us from behind their curtains and wondering who we are,' said Penny. 'The season is over, so we can't be tourists; therefore, what are we doing here? They could be worried that we're estate agents, here to buy up all the houses as second homes for out-of-towners. In which case, it's no wonder they're so suspicious of us.'

'That's all right,' I said. 'I'm suspicious of them.'

We made our way through the complicated maze of twisting streets, some of them so narrow they didn't even have pavements. The houses had a surprisingly similar look to them, for all their period charm, and seemed strangely lacking in character. The old stone frontages stared back at me like so many blank faces, and the windows were like watching eyes. As Penny and I made our way through the town, the streets grew even narrower and the houses seemed to press forward, crowding in around us. We walked through darkening shadows as the lowering cottages blocked out more and more of the light, until it felt as if we were lost and wandering in some old-time woods, with vicious predators lurking somewhere just out of sight.

'If you were any more jumpy, you'd be tying yourself in knots trying to look in every direction at once,' said Penny, carefully not looking at me. 'And that really isn't like you, Ishmael.'

'I don't like the feel of these streets,' I said. 'It's like they're hiding something from us.'

'They seem peaceful enough to me,' said Penny.

'Peaceful as a tomb . . .'

She shuddered briefly and moved a little closer to me. 'You had to go there, didn't you? Are you seeing something that I'm missing?'

'I don't know,' I said. 'What are you seeing?'

Penny took a good look around her. 'Not a damned thing, darling. And I'm not feeling anything either.'

I shrugged. 'I suppose it could just be me . . .'

'No,' Penny said immediately. 'If you say something's not right about this overwhelmingly, appallingly picturesque little town, then I believe you. I'd just feel a lot happier if you had some idea as to what it might be.'

'I thought we were walking into a trap,' I said slowly. 'But now it feels more like we're walking into the lair of some ancient beast. And the beast is hungry.'

Penny looked at me. 'Please tell me that was a metaphor.'

I managed a smile for her. 'Hard to tell.'

'Is any of this seeming at all familiar?' said Penny. In a not at all *I am changing the subject* kind of way. 'Do you recognize any of these streets, from the first time you were here?'

I shook my head. 'Given the confused state I was in, I'm amazed I even remembered the name of the town. In fact . . . the streets here are such a maze, I was lucky to find my way through the town and out the other side. I could have spent hours wandering round and round in circles.'

Penny frowned. 'You were lucky . . .'

'And we don't believe in luck like that,' I said slowly. 'It's almost as if I was guided through the streets.'

'You said the transformation machines downloaded useful information into your head,' said Penny. 'Maybe that included an A-to-Z of the town.'

'Maybe,' I said dubiously. 'But how could they know details like that . . . Unless the ship really was coming here.'

I looked quickly behind me, hoping to catch someone by surprise, but the street was completely devoid of company.

'Stop doing that!' said Penny, staring determinedly straight ahead. 'You're embarrassing me.'

'There's no one here to see you being embarrassed,' I said reasonably.

'Well, if there's no one here, why are you so jumpy? You weren't this nervous when we investigated that haunted house in Bath.'

'It's the town,' I said flatly. 'What did Lucy say? *It didn't want us here . . .*'

Penny nodded reluctantly. 'Thanks a whole bunch. Now I am starting to feel something.'

'As though we're walking through a minefield?'

'More like we're mice in a maze, chasing after some cheese that might not even be there.'

'In which case,' I said, 'whose maze is it?'

Penny glared at me. 'Congratulations, Ishmael. You have managed to find the exact phrase to make me feel even more disturbed.'

'It's a gift,' I said modestly.

The town hospital turned out to be one of those old-fashioned cottage hospitals you used to see in black-and-white films on BBC Two in the afternoon. The kind that haven't actually existed for ages. It all added to the growing feeling of unreality, as though I was walking through someone else's dream.

The car park was completely empty. No sign of an ambulance or even a paramedic's motorbike, and not a single visitor's car. There weren't even any designated parking bays for the doctors. Just an open space, as if someone had meant to put something there but never got round to it. Penny and I paused at the entrance, so we could study the hospital. The one and only door remained firmly closed, as though the hospital wanted to make it clear we were not at all welcome.

A small, illuminated sign over the door said simply, *Hospital*. As if someone wasn't even trying. Because now we were this close, it didn't matter any more. It was all very still, with not a sound anywhere, and I was starting to find that just a bit sinister.

'It's quiet,' I said solemnly. 'Too quiet.'

'Stop it, darling,' said Penny. 'You are really not helping.'

'Sorry,' I said. 'I felt it was expected of me. Besides, it is too quiet. No people, no traffic, no birdsong . . . Not even the murmur of a passing breeze.'

'OK . . .' said Penny. 'That really isn't normal. What do you think is going on here?'

'I think we're supposed to believe this is just an ordinary little country town. But it isn't. It feels more to me like we've booked into a hotel and discovered it's only a doll's house – and we're the next toys to be played with.'

Penny looked at me. 'Where did that come from?'

'Damned if I know,' I said. 'Nothing in this town is anything like what I expected. We came here to solve one mystery and seem to have walked into another.'

'Oh, good,' said Penny. 'As if we didn't have enough on our plate.' She shifted her feet uncomfortably. 'How much longer are we going to stand around, being ostentatiously conspicuous?'

'Until someone notices,' I said. 'In fact, I'm surprised someone hasn't come out of the hospital to ask us what we're doing here.'

I raised my voice for that last bit, letting my words ring clearly across the open space, but no one emerged from the hospital to challenge us. The closed front door stared defiantly back, as though daring us to try something.

'Well?' said Penny. 'Are we going in?'

'And walk right into the lion's jaws?' I said. 'I don't think so.'

'But isn't that what we came here for?' said Penny. 'To get in people's faces and ask questions?'

'We can't just pop in and demand access to their mortuary,' I said patiently. 'Because we don't have Organization authority to back us up. So I suggest we take a little wander around the hospital exterior and see what there is to see.'

'Like a side door we can persuade to open, so we can sneak in?'

I smiled at her. 'Being around me has taught you so much.'

We set out across the open space of the car park, like hunters venturing into a jungle clearing. It wasn't long before we found a small but prominent sign, pointing the way to the mortuary.

'How very useful,' I said.

'And almost insultingly obvious,' said Penny.

'As if someone wanted to make sure we didn't miss it.'

'There is always the chance that sign wasn't meant for us, specifically,' said Penny. 'A maze doesn't care which mice get trapped in it.'

'I'd feel happier if this was just a trap,' I said. 'I know how to deal with traps.'

'Walk right in and smash everything up?' said Penny.

'Always works for me.'

We followed the sign's directions, round the side of the hospital.

'If there is a body in the mortuary,' said Penny, 'and it does turn out to be Vincent Smith, what do we do then? Turn around and go home?'

I looked at her. 'You think that's what we should do?'

'Whatever plan you might once have had, it is currently sitting in a corner banging its head against the wall,' said Penny. 'It's not like there's anyone else we can talk to, to give us the kind of answers we were hoping to get from Smith. Always assuming he really was what you thought he was. And if we really have walked into some carefully constructed trap, we might be better off just quietly backing out of it. We can always come back another time, in force and better prepared.'

'We are not leaving this town until I have some idea of what's going on,' I said. 'Smith may be a dead end, but there are still questions to be asked and answers to be found. Starting with: if Vincent Smith is dead, who killed him? And did they know what, as well as who, they were killing?'

'We don't know for sure that anyone killed him,' Penny said stubbornly. 'Old people die of heart attacks all the time.'

'You don't believe that any more than I do,' I said.

'The timing is suspicious,' Penny admitted.

'I'm starting to wonder whether my investigation might have drawn attention to Smith's existence,' I said. 'I'd hate to think I was responsible for his death.'

'Stop that right now,' Penny said sharply. 'How could your enemies have known about Vincent Smith? We only know because the confidential report named him as a Person of Interest.'

'Maybe Black Heir told them,' I said.

Penny looked at me, shocked. 'Why would they do that?'

'You can't profit from as many crashed alien ships as they do and not develop certain useful relationships,' I said. 'It's always possible that someone at Black Heir made a deal.'

'With certain useful people?'

'Not necessarily people.'

'Aliens?'

'Or their agents.'

Penny thought about that. 'Did you ever meet any other aliens when you were working for Black Heir?'

'No,' I said. 'If there was contact, it took place at much higher levels than I had access to. But there were always rumours. You have to understand: a lot of the subterranean groups base their structure on the old Russian doll – several increasingly smaller dolls, stacked inside each other. So you end up with groups within groups, and departments within departments that don't officially exist. The left hand never knowing how the right hand is stacking the deck. Black Heir was created to perform a function, but it's been around so long it couldn't help but accumulate all kinds of other interests and hidden agendas.'

'You really think Black Heir might be responsible for Smith's death?'

I shrugged. 'Or any of the other underground groups, if they thought they had a good reason to keep him from talking to me.'

'Like what?' said Penny.

'Depends on what Smith knew,' I said. 'Or what they thought he knew. It's always possible my investigation spooked Smith into reaching out to one of these groups, looking for protection, and it all went horribly wrong.'

'OK,' said Penny. 'You're reaching now. The investigation didn't turn up any evidence that Smith moved in the same world as we do. Lucy was quite emphatic about that.'

'Yes,' I said. 'I wonder why she felt the need to make such a point of it.'

Penny shook her head. 'How could a small-time, small-town author like Vincent Smith come into contact with our kind of people?'

'Maybe he didn't hide his true nature as successfully as he thought,' I said. 'We found him easily enough. Other people could have come here looking for him, for all kinds of reasons. Some of the subterranean groups have pretty weird interests.' I stopped and frowned. 'Like the British Psychic Weapons Division and their obsession with security. What if Mr Nemo didn't find the information about Vincent Smith inside my head? What if he already knew and only put it in my head when it would be most advantageous to his group?'

Penny looked at me for a long moment. 'You're saying we can't trust anybody?'

'Now you're getting the hang of things.'

'What if Black Heir wasn't invited into your investigation,' Penny said slowly. 'What if they already knew something – about Smith or you or the ship – and used that leverage to force their way in? That could be why Lucy's here! To keep an eye on us, until she's figured out how much we know about the situation.'

I smiled at her. 'You see? You can be just as paranoid and distrustful as me when you put your mind to it.'

We found the mortuary right at the back of the hospital. Just a blunt square building, standing a little apart from the hospital, with another very basic sign over the door to identify it. A simple box of a building, just waiting to be opened.

'A town this small shouldn't have its own hospital,' I said, 'never mind its own mortuary.'

'Just be grateful it's here,' said Penny. 'If they'd sent the body to some other town, we would have had to go chasing off after it.'

'Yes,' I said. 'It's almost as though someone doesn't want us to leave town now that we're here.'

There was still no one else about, but Penny lowered her voice anyway as she leaned in close.

'You think this is the trap?'

'Smith's body would make the perfect bait,' I said. 'But you need people to spring a trap, and I'm not seeing, hearing or smelling any bad guys lurking in the vicinity.'

Penny smiled at me fondly. 'You and your alien senses. Well, then . . . are we going in or are we just going to stand around making up our minds? The day isn't getting any younger.'

'Let's do it,' I said. 'Everything forward and trust in the Lord, and see what happens. Get ready to stand behind me.'

'You make an excellent human shield,' said Penny. 'If only you were just a bit wider . . .'

The mortuary door was locked. I checked to make sure there weren't any security cameras and then put my shoulder to it. The door ripped itself right out of the splintered wooden frame, leaving rather more evidence of our being there than I was happy with, but I wasn't in the mood to be subtle.

One short, whitewashed corridor later, we were in a small reception area, complete with desk, but there was no one there to man it and no one waiting. The whole place was deathly quiet. I looked quickly around and then frowned at the blank walls.

'Shouldn't there be posters? You know, *Safety in the workplace*, *Wash your hands* and *Please don't cough on the staff* . . . all the usual stuff. For a professional medical setting, this seems disturbingly lacking in details. Like a set that hasn't been properly dressed yet.'

'You've lost me there,' said Penny.

I started to explain my theory of how unreal and staged everything felt, but gave up halfway through. It sounded unconvincing even as I said it.

'Why would anyone go to such lengths?' said Penny.

'Damned if I know,' I said. 'But it's bothering the hell out of me.'

I called out, but no one answered. I picked up the single phone on the desk and put it to my ear, half expecting a silent prop and the sound of the sea, but the dial tone was reassuringly normal. I replaced the receiver and then drummed my fingertips on it thoughtfully.

'I'm not seeing any computer,' said Penny. 'How do they make appointments and access patient records?'

'Maybe someone removed it,' I said, 'because it had important information about Vincent Smith.'

Penny scowled around her. 'Where the hell are the staff? It's starting to feel like the Pied Piper just breezed through and abducted everybody.'

'I'm sure there's a perfectly reasonable explanation,' I said.

Penny looked at me. 'Honestly?'

'No, probably not,' I said. 'I just needed to say that out loud, to see if I could convince myself.'

'And?' said Penny.

'Not even close,' I said. 'Follow me.'

I vaulted over the reception desk and then put out a hand to assist Penny, but she just glared at me coldly until I took it away. She slipped over the desk in one smooth movement, and I gestured at the door behind the counter. Penny raised an eyebrow.

'You're sure this leads to the actual mortuary?'

'I can smell industrial-strength disinfectant beyond it,' I said.

Penny nodded. 'After you, space boy.'

'Stick close, spy girl.'

I listened carefully at the closed door and then quickly kicked it open, but there was no one lying in wait. Penny let me do all of that without any comment, which was a sign of just how tense she was getting. Ahead of us lay another short corridor, with another door at the end. I was ready to smash that in too, but it wasn't locked. I didn't wait to decide whether that was suspicious; I just slammed the door open and strode in, ready for anything, with Penny right behind me.

The mortuary was all white-tiled walls, steel trays with medical instruments, and a really powerful smell of disinfectant. The single examination slab had no body on it. The only dead body was lying on the floor beside the slab, and he didn't look anything like Vincent Smith. Barely middle-aged, in a smart dark suit, the dead man's face was entirely unfamiliar. Penny and I stared at him for a long moment.

'One of the mortuary staff?' Penny said finally.

'He's not wearing a white coat,' I said.

'Do they wear white coats in a mortuary?'

'I kind of feel they should.'

I knelt down beside the body and looked it over carefully.

'No obvious injuries,' I said finally. 'No blood, no defensive wounds that would indicate he put up a struggle. Nothing in his face to suggest a heart attack. It's as though he just walked in here and dropped down dead.'

'Could it have been shock?' said Penny. 'Because he saw something he wasn't supposed to? Like Vincent Smith coming back to life, sitting up on the slab and smiling at him?'

'That would do it,' I said. I got to my feet again and sniffed at the air. 'I can't pick up anyone else's scent – not past all this disinfectant.' I concentrated, listening hard. 'But I am definitely not hearing anyone else, anywhere in the building.'

'Alien,' said Penny. 'Is there any way you can tell whether Smith's body was ever here?'

I leaned right over until my face was almost level with the slab and then inhaled deeply.

'Oh, ick,' said Penny.

'Someone was here,' I said. 'I'm picking up . . .'

'Really don't want to know!' Penny said loudly. 'Just tell me: were they actually dead?'

'There are scents I would associate with death.'

Penny waited and then raised an eyebrow. 'That's it?'

'Afraid so.'

'All right, then . . . Could someone have broken in here before us and stolen Smith's body?'

'It's possible,' I said. 'I'll search the room for clues; you check the dead man's pockets. See if there's anything to tell us who he was.'

Penny nodded quickly, knelt down beside the body and rummaged through his clothes with practised thoroughness. She'd been my partner on enough murder cases that such things didn't bother her any more. I moved slowly round the room, looking for anything out of place.

There wasn't enough there for anything to be out of place. Just like the outer office, the mortuary room held nothing but the bare essentials. There was no way a standard autopsy could have been carried out. They simply didn't have the equipment. Perhaps this was just a holding area – somewhere to store a body until it could be transported to a better-equipped mortuary in another town.

'I've got a wallet and a driving licence,' said Penny. 'That gives us a name: Winston Almond. And here's a business card . . . Ishmael, he was the town's funeral director.'

'Someone must have called him in,' I said. 'But isn't it a bit previous to summon an undertaker before there's even been an autopsy?'

'Maybe that's why someone had to remove Smith's body in a hurry,' said Penny. 'If he was poisoned to give the appearance of a heart attack, an undertaker might have noticed something.'

'There's got to be more to this than a simple poisoning,' I said.

Penny tucked the wallet back where she had found it and got to her feet. 'What else could kill a man and leave no obvious clues? I mean, every weapon leaves some trace.'

'Not necessarily,' I said.

Penny looked at me sharply. 'You know something.'

'I know lots of things,' I said. 'Not all of them pleasant. Back when I was with Black Heir, we found all kinds of useful tech in crashed alien ships. Once, I found a very interesting weapon. All you had to do was point it at someone, and they dropped dead without a mark on them.'

'How did you find that out?' said Penny.

'Exactly how you think,' I said. 'In any job, there are always accidents in the workplace. But that couldn't have been what killed Smith. There was only the one weapon, and I destroyed it.'

'Well done you,' said Penny.

'I didn't trust Black Heir, even then.'

'Someone could have found another one.'

'I'm pretty sure I would have heard if something like that was being used,' I said. 'Spies gossip like teenage girls over a new boyfriend. But it is definitely suspicious that a Black Heir agent should come to town just as people start dying mysteriously.'

'You think Lucy . . .?'

'That feels a bit too obvious,' I said. 'More likely she was sent here as a distraction, to keep us from noticing what else is going on.'

'You think there could be other agents operating in the town?' said Penny.

'Wouldn't surprise me.'

I stared thoughtfully at the empty slab.

'Could Smith have come back to life?' I said. 'And then killed Almond so he couldn't tell anyone?'

'Or maybe someone came in here to steal Smith's body and then killed Almond when he turned up.'

'Why would he do that?'

'Panic? Or because he couldn't leave a witness behind who might have been able to identify him.' Penny stopped and frowned. 'Of course, that does rather beg the question, why would anyone want to take Smith's body in the first place?'

'There's a whole underground market when it comes to alien tissues and DNA,' I said. 'Sometimes you need them to make alien tech or weapons work. Sometimes they can tell us things about what it's like out there. And alien chemicals can always lead to useful new drugs. There's lots of money to be made from dead aliens. Just another reason why I prefer to keep my true nature secret.'

'But if Smith had been made completely human by the transformation machines . . .'

'Maybe someone thought there would be clues on the body that could lead them to the buried starship.'

'But who else would know about the ship?'

'The ones who shot it down,' I said.

Penny looked at me sharply. 'You think your enemies might already be here, in the town?'

'Remember the Case of the Missing Mummy,' I said. 'The enemy can possess people.'

Penny's mouth made a shocked *Oh* of understanding.

'Is that why everyone's been acting the way they have?'

'The aliens couldn't have possessed the whole town,' I said. 'That would have set off alarms in every underground group there is. Very definitely including the Organization and Black Heir. They have systems in place to pick up on things like mass possession.' I shook my head. 'Come on, let's go, before someone catches us here with Almond and draws all the wrong conclusions.'

'We're just going to leave him lying on the floor?' said Penny.

'You want me to put him on the slab?' I said. 'Trust me: he doesn't care. He's dead.'

FOUR
Local Hospitality

The mortuary door wasn't in the mood to shut, because of what I'd done to it earlier, so I left it hanging open. Penny and I moved quickly back to the front of the hospital, and we were almost halfway across the car park when the hospital's front door suddenly swung open. Caught out in the open, Penny and I had no choice but to stand where we were and try to look as if we had every right to be there. A woman patient slowly emerged from the open door, wearing one of those flimsy hospital gowns that does up at the back. Bony-faced and hollow-eyed, she looked frail but determined, with an IV drip in her arm connected to one of those steel poles on wheels. I looked at Penny.

'Maybe she's trying to escape.'

'What could be so wrong about the hospital that she'd make a run for it in that condition?' said Penny.

'Maybe we should ask her.'

I was about to start forward when the woman fixed me with a cold look that said, very clearly, *Mind your own business*, so I decided to stay where I was. She came to a halt just outside the hospital door, reached into a breast pocket and brought out a pack of cigarettes and a lighter.

'I get it,' I said to Penny. 'She isn't allowed to smoke inside the hospital, so she's sneaked out here for a quick drag and a cough.'

'I think there's more to it than that . . .' said Penny.

And then we both winced as the woman stuck her cigarette into the tracheotomy hole in her throat and lit up. After a moment, she removed the cigarette and blew a smoke ring in our direction, from out of the hole.

'How is she even doing that?' said Penny in a quietly horrified voice.

'I don't think I want to know,' I said.

The woman shot us a triumphant glance and stuck her cigarette back in the hole. At which point a uniformed nurse appeared in the doorway, looking very relieved to have caught up with her patient. She took hold of the woman's arm and turned her firmly around to take her back inside. And then she glared at Penny and me, as though we'd been encouraging her patient's bad behaviour. I was honestly lost for anything to say. The nurse turned up her nose, and they both went back in.

'You know,' said Penny, 'if I was reduced to smoking through a hole someone had cut in my throat, I would seriously consider quitting. At least, now we know there are people in there.'

'Yes,' I said. 'And they know we're here. Let's hope they don't connect us with the dead body on the mortuary floor, or the body that isn't on the slab.'

Penny caught the tone in my voice and looked at me sharply.

'You think that whole scene was staged just for our benefit?'

'It worked, didn't it?' I said. 'It got us to stand here, out in the open, when we should have been leaving . . . so someone could get a good look at us.'

I stared hard at the hospital windows, but the heavy net curtains blocked my view quite efficiently. I gave them a little wave anyway, to show there were no hard feelings.

'Who is there in the town who'd know we're important enough to go to that much trouble?' Penny said thoughtfully.

'Lucy knows,' I said.

'You think Black Heir ordered her to spread the news?'

'If they're behind what's happening in Norton Hedley,' I said.

'What do you think is happening?' said Penny.

'Damned if I know,' I said. 'But I'm starting to think the whole town is one big trap.'

'That's a lot of trouble to go to, just for us.'

'Maybe it's for anyone who asks too many questions.'

Penny shook her head immediately. 'Your investigating team didn't report any weird reactions.'

'That's right,' I said. 'They didn't. Unless both sets of agents were ordered not to tell us.'

Penny stared at me for a long moment. 'OK, we are now speeding past paranoia and into the land of tinfoil hats and Trust Nobody.'

'I never left,' I said cheerfully. 'Come on, let's get moving. Before they send out a patient with a camera crammed into their eye socket.'

The town seemed emptier than ever. Not a single car on the road, and no one left on the pavements to nod to. I was starting to wonder if the townspeople knew something bad was in the offing, and they were all hiding indoors until it was over. I took Penny by the arm and hurried us along one narrow street after another, cutting quickly back and forth at random. Normally, I would have known if anyone was following us, but the normal rules didn't seem to apply in Norton Hedley. I finally noticed how out of breath Penny was getting, and eased off. She took a moment and then glowered at me.

'Where are we going in such a hurry?'

'Nowhere in particular,' I said. 'Just away from the crime scene.'

'Don't you think we should inform the local police about what's happened?' asked Penny.

'What could we tell them?' I said reasonably. 'We don't know what happened to Smith's body, and we don't know what happened to Almond. All we could say for sure is that we were inside the town mortuary without official permission, for no reason we're prepared to talk about. I don't see that going down very well, do you?'

'Well, when you put it like that . . .'

'We are not here to investigate crimes or solve murders. We're here to dig up the truth about my past.'

'Maybe we need to solve the murders to get to the truth,' said Penny.

'Or maybe we need to concentrate on what matters,' I said.

'That's cold, Ishmael,' said Penny.

I didn't argue, because she was right.

I set off again, allowing Penny to set the pace, but when I took us through another random turn, suddenly we'd left the town behind us and were staring down a narrow path into an open field. It stretched away into the distance – just patchy grass and open ground, abandoned to grow wild. The wood off to one side looked as if it covered quite an area, its tall leafless trees packed close together as though for comfort, or to keep out intruders. The interior seemed to be mostly shadows, deep and dark. I couldn't help feeling that a wood like that, and shadows like that, could be hiding any number of secrets.

'Could this be the field where you first arrived?' said Penny.

I tore my gaze away from the wood. The field had none of the grim foreboding of the trees; it was just an empty place that people no longer visited.

'I don't recognize anything,' I said finally. 'I do remember that the field back then was ploughed, suggesting it had been put to use. This is just open ground. But maybe all the fields around town are like this now.'

'How many are there?' said Penny.

'Quite a few,' I said. 'I studied maps of the area before I left London.'

'Are we going to have to check all of them?' said Penny.

'I intend to look every single one of them in the eye,' I said. 'Until I remember something.'

'Are you getting the same bad feeling here,' Penny said quietly, 'that you were getting on the train, and in the town?'

I fought down an urge to sigh heavily, because I didn't want Penny to think I was impatient with her, given that her question was perfectly reasonable. But I really did feel like a good sigh.

'It's hard for me to get a handle on exactly what it is that I've been feeling. Every time I try to get a grip on what this town is doing to me, it slips away. But it does feel different, out here. It's as if the town presents a real danger, which I haven't identified yet, while the countryside feels like it's hiding something from me.'

Penny looked out across the open field. 'How could anything

be hiding in that? There isn't enough cover out there to conceal a field mouse with a hunchback.'

'Something's here.'

'Maybe your ship's buried under this field!' said Penny. 'And that's what you're feeling . . .'

'No. If my ship was here, I'd know.' I shook my head quickly as I made up my mind. 'We won't find any answers out here. You get answers by asking questions, and for that we need people to browbeat. We are going back into town.'

I turned my back on the field and walked away, and Penny came with me.

And just like that, there were people back in the streets. Just a few, here and there, sticking close together and maintaining a careful distance as they studied Penny and me. Normally, I go to great pains not to be noticed when I'm walking up and down in the world, but I wasn't picking up any sign of a threat. They just seemed . . . interested. And yet I couldn't help feeling there was something off about them. I'm usually pretty good at reading faces; that's part of what keeps an agent safe in enemy territory. But all of the faces watching us looked the same, as though they were all thinking exactly the same thought. And I had no idea what that might be.

'Maybe we should offer to pose for a selfie,' said Penny, just a bit sharply. 'Then they could stare at that, instead of us.'

'I really don't do selfies,' I said.

'Then why don't I just walk up to someone, hit them with my most charming smile and ask them point-blank what the problem is?'

'I think we need to find someone a little more approachable to start with.'

'And where are we going to find someone like that in a town like this?'

'At the Pale Horse,' I said. 'If you want to know a town's history, and its gossip, talk to the hotel staff. They're usually local, and they get to see everyone come and go. We have a room booked, so we have a perfectly good reason to be asking cheerful, innocent questions about what's going on. Anyway, I think we could both use a bit of a rest.'

'Damn right,' said Penny. 'My feet are killing me. If I'd known we were going to be doing this much walking, I'd have gone for more sensible shoes.'

I glanced down at her fashionable footwear and had enough sense not to smile.

'Which part of "We're going to the countryside" did you not pick up on?'

Penny didn't even look at me. 'Don't get snotty, darling.'

There are times when even I can tell it's a good moment to change the subject.

'You'd better try your phone again. We didn't ask Lucy where the hotel is.'

Penny raised her eyes to heaven, as though asking for guidance or patience.

'You didn't think to check that, before we left London?'

'I thought there'd be a taxi.'

Penny gave me a look that said many things, got out her phone and logged on to the town site again.

When we finally arrived at the Pale Horse Hotel, it turned out to be only a few streets away from the railway station. A large three-storey structure, with black Tudor woodwork laid over creamy stone walls, it looked welcoming enough, if somewhat lacking in the character department. Lucy was right: so much effort had gone into making the hotel appear charmingly old-fashioned and tourist-friendly that it had no atmosphere of its own, no sense of place or history. It could have been any small hotel, in any small country town.

Roses had been threaded through wooden frames around the front door, which had been left invitingly open. There was even a hanging sign, like a pub, whose painted image showed a stylized white horse, running across a ploughed field under a full moon. I stopped and studied the sign, while Penny waited patiently. The scene was a little too close to how I'd arrived for my liking. Did someone in this town know about that? About me? Penny stirred at my side, as though she might be about to say something, so I just shrugged internally and led the way in.

The lobby was small, dimly lit and almost overpoweringly

cosy. Mahogany wood-panelled walls gleamed richly in the subdued lighting, and the parquet floor had been polished very recently; I could still smell the wax. Pleasantly inoffensive paintings on the walls, flowers in vases that clearly hadn't been watered lately, a newspaper rack that hadn't been filled – all signs of a tourist trap that hadn't seen a lot of visitors recently. A reception desk took up one end of the lobby, but there was no one around to welcome us.

'Just like the mortuary,' Penny said quietly. 'Doesn't anyone show up for work in this town?'

'Maybe there's a school fair or a garden party going on,' I said.

Penny shook her head firmly. 'I checked the town site. There's nothing listed.'

'Then perhaps they're all gathered together somewhere secluded, building a giant wicker man.'

She smiled at me sweetly. 'That's only for virgins.'

We headed for the reception desk, our feet clattering loudly on the parquet floor. No one emerged to greet us, so Penny and I took a moment to leaf through some helpful brochures scattered across the desk. The cheaply produced pamphlets promoted scenic local walks, historical buildings and sites of interest, and simple introductions to ley lines, UFO sites and haunted hot spots. All in that tiny print that almost defies you to read it, alongside badly cropped photos and amateur illustrations. So far, so as expected. There was an old-fashioned brass bell on the desk, so I struck it smartly, and a loud, rich sound filled the lobby. A voice answered immediately from off to our right.

'Hello, dears! I'm in the snug. Come on through!'

The adjoining bar turned out to be pleasant enough, but the only person in it was a middle-aged woman standing behind the bar and getting stuck into a glass of red wine. From the way she was standing, I guessed it wasn't her first glass. Large and cheerful, in a floral-print dress that could have used some letting out, she smiled at Penny and me with professional hospitality. She was good-looking in an obvious sort of way, with a mess of dark curly hair and far too much makeup: the look of someone determined to make an impression, whatever it took. She made no move to come out from behind the bar, so we went over to join her.

'Welcome to the Pale Horse!' she said grandly. 'I'm Ellie Markham – owner, manager and all that's left of the staff now the season is at an end. Not that it bothers me. I've run this place on my own for more than twenty years, ever since my husband Charlie died. Only helpful thing that man ever did for me. Sorry I wasn't in reception, but there's a lot to do and only me to do it. I take it you're Mr Jones and Ms Belcourt? Glad to have you here! Glad to have anyone, to be honest. You're the only guests staying here, this far out of season. In fact, you're the first new faces I've seen in weeks.'

'Really?' I said, doing my best to get a word in edgeways.

'This is a tourist town, dears – overrun with visitors while the sun shines, then left to our own devices for the rest of the year. So I've been using the spare time to do a spot of stocktaking.'

She lifted her glass unselfconsciously to her lips and drank what was left in one go. She sighed happily and then put the glass down on the bar top as though it wasn't worthy of her attention any more. She looked vaguely around her, as though thinking about a refill, and then remembered she still had guests.

'A lot of the townspeople drink in my bar, now the tourists have gone home. I like to think we provide a social heart for the town. It's important for every small town to have a sense of community. And a full bar does help to keep the hotel solvent, out of season.'

'We booked a room,' I said, as she finally paused for breath. 'I'm afraid we don't have any luggage. Travel light, travel fast – you know how it is.'

'Oh, never mind that, dear,' said Ellie. 'We don't stand on ceremony at the Pale Horse; we just want your money. Pardon my use of the royal "we"; I do so much work around here I tend to think there's more of me than there actually is. Don't worry about the luggage; we can provide you with everything you need. For a price, of course.'

'Oh, of course,' I said.

'Would you like a drink, dears?' Ellie said hopefully. 'Never too early in the day to put a song in your heart and a spring in your step.'

Alcohol has never had any effect on me, but I have found that a little social drinking can do a lot to help when you're trying to get people to open up to you. So I said I'd have a brandy, and a gin and tonic for Penny, and when I asked Ellie to join us, she immediately pushed aside her wine glass and poured herself a large vodka. Penny and I sipped our drinks; Ellie knocked hers back in one. She then told me the price of the drinks, and I did my best not to wince. I told Ellie to add it to the bill, and she smiled happily.

'Out-of-season prices, I'm afraid, dears. So . . . what brings you lovely young people to Norton Hedley this late in the year? Are you interested in the countryside, the history or the weird stuff?'

'Do you get a lot of people interested in that last one?' I said.

'Oh, ever so many, dear,' said Ellie. 'We get the flying saucer people, though apparently we're not supposed to call them that these days; it's all UFOs and close encounters. Then there's the ley line people, who seem perfectly happy to just wander around to no purpose . . . And, of course, there's always the ghost hunters. We have several official ghost walks right here in the town, run by local experts who know all the stories if you're that way inclined. Cold spots available on request.

'This town has always attracted tourists desperate to check out our local colour and fascinating folklore. But, like everything else, it's seasonal. People prefer to indulge their enthusiasms in bright sunshine. It's all a bit different once autumn comes, and the days turn cold and grey. At this time of the year, we're mostly left to our own resources.'

She paused for a moment to look thoughtfully at Penny and me. 'Is there anything in particular that warms the cockles of your hearts, dears? Whatever it is, I'm sure I can put you in touch with someone who knows all about it.'

'We're interested in the UFO that's supposed to have landed here, back in 1963,' I said.

'Oh, yes, dear,' Ellie said immediately. 'We get a lot of

people because of that. It's supposed to have come down somewhere just outside the town. No one's ever found any trace of it, but don't let that stop you from looking! Another drink? No? Don't blame you, at these prices. Don't mind me if I do . . .'

She poured herself another large vodka, which quickly went the way of the first.

'We haven't had anyone staying here for weeks,' she said sadly. 'Not since a whole bunch of people turned up at once, asking all kinds of questions. Some kind of survey, we thought . . . Probably the government, going by their attitude. I was happy to put them up, and between them they took every room in the hotel. Even when it meant doubling up. And they didn't flinch when they heard the room rates. That's what we like here: people on expense accounts. But most of them turned out to be a real pain. Didn't show a bit of interest in the souvenir shops, or the themed cafés . . . They just wanted to ask people questions about all the strange things that are supposed to have happened in the town. At first everyone was happy to talk to them, given that the weird stuff is our bread and butter, so to speak. The word going around was that these people might be doing research for a television show, and we all liked the sound of that, but they didn't exactly make themselves popular.'

'Why?' said Penny. 'What did they do?'

'It was their attitude, you see, dears. All *we know better than you*. Questions, questions, questions – and never satisfied with the answers they got. They were really rude, sometimes, in the way they challenged everything. And everyone here doing their best to be helpful, telling the stories they've been telling tourists for generations. We were all of us glad to see the back of them in the end. And you should have seen the mess they made of my rooms! Some people are just pigs once they get away from home.'

I was remembering Lucy telling Penny and me that everyone in the investigating team had been too spooked to stay in the town overnight. Which made me wonder why Lucy didn't want us staying at the Pale Horse. I realized Ellie was staring at me.

'We've seen a few of the locals,' I said. 'They didn't seem too friendly.'

'Oh, don't take it personally, dear,' said Ellie. 'I think everyone's just a bit questioned out, at the moment.'

'Why haven't we seen many people?' I said. 'Where is everybody?'

Ellie gave me an odd look. 'They're all at work, dear. Hardly anyone has a job in the town, out of season. They all go off to work in the cities, where the money is. But don't you worry, dear; the bar will be packed full by this evening, and you'll have as much company as you can stand!'

'That sounds more like it,' I said. 'Perhaps people will be feeling more friendly by then.'

'They will if you're buying the drinks,' Ellie said cheerfully. 'They can be a real thirsty crowd around here.'

'Do you think we could see our room now?' said Penny. 'Only I would like to put my feet up for a while.'

'Of course, dear!' said Ellie.

She emerged from behind the bar, revealing that she was wearing pink stiletto heels to raise herself to average height. She escorted us back into the lobby, settled herself comfortably behind the reception desk and then gestured grandly at the rows of old-fashioned keys hanging on the wall.

'Take your choice of any room in the hotel, dears. Front, back or next to the stairs. No lift. There are some really nice views from the top floor, if you like woods.'

'That will do nicely,' I said. 'Any extra charge for the view?'

Ellie laughed, which I noted wasn't actually a no, and turned away to search through the keys. While she was busy doing that, I leaned in close to Penny.

'No other guests in the hotel, and no visitors in the town,' I said quietly. 'No wonder we stood out.'

'And the Organization and Black Heir agents seem to have made a right dog's breakfast of their investigation,' said Penny. 'What were they thinking?'

'I shall have some harsh words to say about that, when we get back,' I said. 'Black Heir throwing their weight around like a bull in a china shop – that I can understand – but the Organization is supposed to be more subtle. If the original team have pissed in the waters, we could have a really hard time getting answers out of the locals.'

Penny smiled brightly. 'Then we'll just have to win them over with our sparkling charm and personality.'

'I think I'll leave that to you,' I said.

Ellie finally presented us with the key to room 307. 'You'll like this one, dears. It's very clean.'

'Do you know a local author called Vincent Smith?' I said. 'He wrote a book about the UFO we're interested in.'

'Oh, yes, dear!' said Ellie. 'I've known Vincent for ages. Lovely man. Such a shame . . . You do know he died, just the other day?'

'Yes,' said Penny. 'We're very disappointed. We were hoping to talk to him about his books.'

'I'm sure you'll find someone else who can tell you what you want to know,' said Ellie.

'Were you and Mr Smith close?' I asked.

'Hard to say, dear,' said Ellie. 'We spent a lot of time in each other's company, because he did love to prop up my bar most evenings. My snug has always been the favourite place for visitors to get together and chat about what they're interested in. And Vincent was always ready to pontificate about the weird stuff. He didn't specialize, like most of our visitors. If it was in any way out of the ordinary, you could be sure Vincent knew all about it, and he had proper thought-out opinions on everything. Strange, really, given that he wasn't a local man. He didn't grow up with the weird stuff, like the rest of us did. Perhaps that's why he found it all so fascinating.'

She paused, smiling reflectively. 'I used to love seeing him take his favourite seat at the end of the bar, and then just sit there, drink in hand, and entertain the crowd for hours. I could always be sure of an evening's profit when Vincent was in the chair.'

'Have you read his books?' said Penny.

'Oh, I'm not much of a reader, dear,' said Ellie. 'Though I always told Vincent, "If they ever make a movie out of one of your books, I'll watch that!" But I can't say we were close . . . I knew him for years, but there was always a distance to the man. It was like he was so interested in *things* that there wasn't a lot of room left in him to be interested in people. He liked people, don't get me wrong – he was always friendly – but you couldn't get close to him. He wouldn't let you. Have you read his books?'

'Oh, yes,' said Penny.

'What, all of them?' said Ellie. 'He wrote dozens of the things. I admire your stamina, that's all I can say.'

'We came a long way to talk to him about his work,' I said.

'Oh, bless; he would have liked that.'

'You said he wasn't local?' said Penny.

'No, dear,' said Ellie. 'You have to be born right here in the town to be local. Vincent came to live in Norton Hedley when he was a young man, back in the sixties. He said he'd read about this town and all the strange stuff that happened here, and couldn't think of anywhere else he'd rather be. He bought a cottage on the edge of town, and just settled in and made himself at home. He'd talk to anyone with a story, whether it was their own or something that had been passed down through the family, and then he'd polish it up and put it in one of his books. No one ever objected. We all knew it was good for the town. And to be honest, he could make a good story out of practically anything. You'd hardly recognize some of the old tales after he was through with them.

'The research that man did . . . He spent ages searching out the exact location for every story, and checking all the facts to make sure they fitted together properly. Which is more than a lot of the original storytellers did. You won't be offended, I hope, if I hint that not all the local stories are one hundred per cent what actually happened . . . No, I thought not. You look a bit more sophisticated than most of the visitors we get.'

She smiled wistfully, remembering. 'Vincent spent years wandering through the town, and the fields, and the wood . . . immersing himself in the town's history. He always used to say, the devil is in the details. Which was a bit odd, really, because we've never been into Satanism here. That's more your big-city thing.'

'He lived alone?' I said.

'He seemed happy that way,' said Ellie. 'No wife, no family – just a well-respected local scholar who kept himself to himself.' She leaned forward across the reception desk and lowered her voice conspiratorially, even though there was no one else around. 'There were any number of women who would have been only too happy to keep him company, if you catch my drift, but none of them ever got anywhere. He was always polite, don't get me wrong, but as far as I know, he never got involved with anyone. I think he just lived for what interested him. Men are like that, sometimes. Like my Charlie, with his golf . . . It starts out as a hobby, and the next thing you know, it's taken over their lives.

'And now Vincent's gone . . . Makes me feel a bit sad, knowing I'll never listen to him holding forth in the bar again, with the crowd in the palm of his hand. There was no one like him when it came to filling my bar with paying customers.'

I was amazed at how ordinary a life Smith had led. He just came to Norton Hedley, made himself a part of the community and fitted right in. They never had any idea he was anything other than what he appeared to be. It was as though Smith had learned how to be fully human, while I never had.

'Did he have any close friends?' I said. 'Anyone we could talk to about his work?'

'I know who you want,' said Ellie. 'You want Frank Kendall, the town librarian. They were always close. And equally absorbed in the weird stuff.'

She leaned forward over the desk again, her conspiratorial glance inviting Penny and me to lean in closer, so she could dispense the good stuff. Her breath had so much alcohol on it you could have set light to it.

'Some of us did wonder whether the two of them might have been a bit closer than that, on the quiet. I mean, we all know Frank is gay – even if he's never actually come out and said it, because most people wouldn't approve. Small town – you know how it is. But if there ever was anything between them, no one ever saw it. And I don't think there was. Like I said, Vincent lived for his work.'

'Where can we find Frank?' said Penny.

'At the town library,' said Ellie. 'We've still got one, though the council keeps threatening to shut it down to save money. But that'll never happen. Frank has made our little library a haven for any tourist with a taste for the weird stuff. He has books and pamphlets and all kinds of stuff you wouldn't believe. Frank and his collection are a major tourist attraction and bring a lot of money into the town.'

'And you think he'd be happy to talk to us?' said Penny. 'About Vincent and his books?'

'Oh, he's always happy to talk, is Frank,' said Ellie. 'The library doesn't get many visitors out of season.'

'Because people around here aren't great readers?' I said.

'Bang on target, dear! You trot along now and talk to Frank, if you can get a word in. He'll talk your back leg off, that one will, given half a chance. You just ask him about Vincent, and he'll be happy to tell you whatever it is you need to know. Because he's like that.'

She gave us directions to the library, without having to be asked. It wasn't far.

'Give Frank my best,' said Ellie. 'You will be nice to him, won't you? That last bunch gave him a bit of a hard time. Always trying to bully more details out of him, or take bits of his collection out of the library. As if he'd ever let them go. Some of the visitors called him a fool to his face, just because he likes to believe in some of the stranger stuff even when there isn't any real evidence. He had to throw them out of his library in the end, and ban them from coming back. And it takes a lot to get on Frank's bad side.'

'Perhaps we shouldn't disturb him,' said Penny, 'if he's upset over his friend's death?'

'Oh, no, dear, you go and see him,' Ellie said firmly. 'He could use some company. And he'll be glad of someone he can show off his collection to. Everyone around here has seen it.' She sighed. 'He's been the town librarian all his working life. Runs the place single-handed. Practically lives there. But . . . he's getting on. Someday he'll be forced to retire, and that will break his heart.'

FIVE

Talking to the Man Who Knows

The library was easy enough to find, but we didn't expect it to be tucked away in the shadow of a Restoration-period mansion house. A tall and sprawling structure, the mansion's grey stone walls were covered in thick mats of creeping ivy; the roof was crowded with arching gables, and seriously ugly gargoyles sneered out at the world. Every single window was full of darkness, like so many suspicious eyes.

'Why didn't Ellie mention this?' said Penny.

'Probably thought we'd notice it soon enough for ourselves,' I said.

'Big, isn't it?' said Penny. 'What's it doing right in the middle of town?'

'Maybe this part of town was built around it.'

I made a mental note to ask the librarian about the history of the old mansion, and then ignored it so I could concentrate on the library. The long, thin bungalow with its flat roof seemed to crouch in the shadow of the massive house, as though trying not to be noticed. The door opened easily at my touch, and I led the way in.

'Why do you always insist on going first?' said Penny.

'So I can stand between you and all harm.'

'I can look after myself.'

'I know. I've seen you do it. It's just that I was raised in an older, more chivalrous time.'

'When women knew their place?'

'Not the women I knew . . . OK, let's not go there. The next time we're walking into danger, you can take the lead.'

'What kind of dangers are you expecting in a library?'

'I don't know. That's why I'm going first.'

The brightly lit interior was packed full of bookshelves, set so close together there was hardly any room left to navigate between them. The tall stacks were crammed full of books, squeezed in so tightly it looked as if you'd need a shoehorn to wrestle one out. The librarian appeared to be doing his best to cram as much literature and learning as he could into the limited space provided. But for all the miles of books and associated clutter, the library still managed a cheerful, even cosy ambience. A haven of peace and civilization in an overly commercial town.

Posters on the walls advertised the usual local groups and activities, as well as suggesting places of interest for the inquisitive visitor, but my eyes were drawn to a really big poster from *The X-Files*. The classic image of the UFO, with the legend *I Want to Believe*. Somebody was making a statement.

Penny and I made our way carefully through the maze of bookshelves and, just as Ellie had said, there wasn't a single other soul around. We finally ended up at the main desk, where the librarian was sorting through a pile of old Dennis Wheatley *Library of the Occult* paperbacks. He looked up quickly as Penny and I emerged from the bookshelves, and immediately rose to his feet. He bustled out from behind his desk to greet us, nodding happily as we introduced ourselves.

Frank Kendall had a gentle gaze and a diffident handshake. A tall, slender figure in his late sixties, he wore faded blue jeans and a vintage *Outer Limits* T-shirt. His long grey hair was pulled back in a neat ponytail, and his thin face was offset by round John Lennon glasses. He had the air of a relaxed and entirely unrepentant hippy.

'Welcome to my kingdom of knowledge,' he said. 'What brings you good people here?'

'Ellie sent us,' I said.

Frank nodded quickly. 'Of course. She can always tell when visitors are genuinely interested in what I have to tell them. Kneel at my feet, and I shall dispense the secrets of the ages.'

'I don't really do the kneeling thing,' I said.

'Suit yourself,' Frank said easily. 'But you don't know what you're missing. I am the fount of all wisdom in Norton Hedley. Because somebody has to be.'

'We came here because we're interested in the book Vincent Smith wrote about the 1963 UFO incident,' said Penny.

Frank brightened at the mention of Smith's name. 'You've come to the right place and the right person. No one knew Vincent better than me. Sit down and take the weight off your preconceptions.'

He gathered together three cheap plastic chairs, and after we'd all settled ourselves more or less comfortably, Frank looked inquiringly at Penny and me.

'What knowledge about travellers from distant worlds can I help you with, my bright-eyed young seekers after truth?'

'I hope we're not taking you away from your work,' I said.

He shrugged easily. 'This is it – such as it is.'

'Ellie said you don't get many people in here,' said Penny.

'We do in the summer,' said Frank, just a bit defensively. 'We get lots of visitors while the tourist season is on. I like to think my little library has earned itself a good reputation among the various true believers. And, of course, I have my own website, all about the town and its many stories and legends. We get lots of hits. Though I don't read the comments any more; there are some very hurtful people out there.'

'What about the locals?' I said. 'Aren't they interested?'

'Not so much,' Frank admitted. 'They're all very proud of the library, and they go out of their way to tell me that. They love the tourist money it brings in . . . But the people around here spend so much time selling the local legends to visitors that they don't even want to think about it on their time off. I get them while they're children, of course. They can't get enough of the place . . . But they grow up so quickly and leave all of this behind. Most of the time, it's pretty quiet here. I don't mind. Just gives me more freedom to get on with my research. Always something new to learn about the town's weird history!'

'Penny and I are great admirers of Vincent Smith's books,' I said. 'We were very sorry to hear about his recent death.'

Frank's gentle smile disappeared, and he slumped a little in his chair. For the first time, he looked his age. 'Yes, it was very sudden. But not entirely unexpected.' His smile returned as he looked around at the stacks. 'I like to think he's still here. I have all his books, you know. Personally inscribed and covering a surprisingly wide variety of subjects. That man was interested in anything even a little bit off the beaten track.'

'Were the two of you close?' said Penny.

'Vincent was a good friend to me,' said Frank. 'The best and the smartest man I ever knew. An old soul, I always thought, and a deep one. There was no one else I could talk to like him. It genuinely never mattered to Vincent that I was gay, and there's not a lot of people around here I can say that about.' He shook his head slowly. 'I keep looking up, expecting him to come wandering in as always, ready for a nice cup of tea and a sit down and a chat . . .' Frank forgot about Penny and me for a moment, his gaze lost in the past, and then his gentle smile returned. 'I spent most of my life helping him research this town and all the cool and groovy stories that have accumulated around it down the years.'

'Do you know why he was so interested in the weird stuff?' said Penny.

Frank's smile widened. 'Isn't everybody? Or, at least, everyone worth knowing.' His gaze became vague again as he peered back into his memories. 'I first got interested when I was a teenager. I'd grown up with all the weird stuff, like everyone else, but I thought they were just stories . . . Until I read this book about ley lines. They were all the rage back in the seventies. The hidden paths and secret ways of old England, connecting forgotten places of ancient power. Ley lines maintain the spiritual energies that bind this country and its people together, and to walk them is to open your mind to all the lost wonders of the world. Two major ley lines cross right in the middle of Norton Hedley, not far from where we are. This must have been a location of great power and significance, way back when – perhaps even a place of pilgrimage. Not like now, of course.

'Anyway . . . ley lines led me to study local history, and I was amazed to discover how even the strangest legends often turned out to be based on years of properly accredited sightings. Like Black Shuck, the huge dog with no head who runs endlessly round the borders of the town at night, protecting it from outside threats. Seeing him with your own eyes is supposed to be good luck. Or bad. Not something you'd want to get wrong, really . . . And then there's the recurring ghostly vision of Murdstone Manse, which used to stand on the outskirts of the town. People keep seeing it all over the town, even though it was burned down by the townspeople centuries ago. And for very good reasons, according to some sources.'

'What reasons?' I said.

'Oh, the usual. Demonology and witchcraft, people who'd gone missing under suspicious circumstances . . . All of which stopped once the house was gone and the family with it.'

'I wanted to ask about all the people who've gone missing around here,' I said.

Some of the enthusiasm left Frank's face as he nodded slowly. 'Yes, that is one of the town's darker aspects. I've seen records of unexplained disappearances that go back centuries.'

'So it's not just young people running away to find fame and fortune in the big city?' said Penny.

Frank shook his head firmly. 'The missing include young and old and everyone in between. Perfectly ordinary people who just suddenly aren't around any more. It doesn't happen all that often, just enough to be a worry to those of us who take an interest in these things. People here don't like to talk about it – their way of coping, I suppose. Vincent did start to write a book about the phenomenon, and that was the only time I ever saw the town turn against him. In the end, Vincent quietly abandoned the book.'

'How do you feel about that?' I said.

Frank shrugged briefly, his gentle smile suddenly touched with melancholy.

'It's never wise to makes waves in a small town. It wasn't as though we had any answers to offer, or even a new way of looking at the information. So why upset the feelings of people who'd lost loved ones?'

He pushed the thought aside, and his face brightened again. 'But why dwell on the unpleasant, oh my brethren, when there are so many marvellous mysteries to consider? Norton Hedley is just packed full of wild strangeness and glimpses into the infinite. It's a much bigger world than most people realize.

Vincent did his best to open people's minds to that, with his research and his books. There's so much to see, he always used to say, if people would only open their eyes and look.'

He cocked his head a little to one side, and studied Penny and me with bright, eager eyes.

'Have you checked out the wood that borders our town yet? Oh, you really should, little brother and sister! It has such an intriguing atmosphere, even in broad daylight.'

'We'll take a look, if we have time,' I said politely.

'Vincent always intended to write a book about that wood,' said Frank. 'He was a great one for making connections and demonstrating new ways of looking at old things. But his real obsession was the meteor that so many townspeople saw in the night skies over Norton Hedley, back in 1963.'

'That's why we're here,' I said. 'We read Vincent Smith's book and decided we just had to come and see for ourselves.'

Frank nodded happily. 'A lot of people feel that way. I'm surprised it isn't a better-known story, like Rendlesham. But the problem is, when you get right down to it, there's no evidence. No landing site, no signs of a crash; nothing to indicate that it was ever anything more than just a brighter than usual meteor.' And then he stopped and grinned slyly. 'Though there are some who saw the light flying over the town and swore it changed direction. A meteor doesn't do that.'

'Did you see it?' said Penny.

'Oh, I would have loved that!' said Frank. 'But I was just a young thing back then, fast asleep in bed. My dad saw it, streaking from one side of town to the other. He was convinced it started to come down, somewhere out by the wood. He actually braced himself for the impact, but in the end there wasn't one.'

'I'm sorry,' said Penny, 'but if this all took place in the early hours of the morning, what was your father doing up at such an hour to see it?'

'I asked him that,' said Frank. 'Apparently, before anyone saw anything, there was a really big sound – from somewhere high up in the sky. Loud enough and strange enough to get a lot of people out of their beds and into the streets, to see what was going on.' He stopped and smiled. 'I like to think of them all, standing there in their pyjamas and dressing gowns, craning their heads back to watch a miracle taking place in the night.

'Dad was all for going out into the wood, to search for whatever might have come down, but no one seemed particularly keen to go stumbling around in the dark . . . And after thinking about it for a bit, neither was my dad. The wood's not a good place to be after dark. Once it was light, he managed to shame a few friends into going with him to take a look, but they never found anything.

'All kinds of people have come here since, looking for proof. There isn't a part of the wood where some tourist hasn't claimed to have seen or felt something . . . But for all the photos and videos they take, it's always just trees. In fact, someone filmed a walk through the wood from one end to the other and put it on YouTube, as a kind of virtual tour.'

'Have you seen it?' I said.

'Oh, yes,' said Frank. 'It's just trees.'

'Don't you ever worry that the woods will get overrun?' I said. 'Perhaps even damaged by so many visitors?'

Frank shook his head. 'Most tourists stick to the town, to giggle at the better-known stories and spend their money on the usual touristy things. The wood is a bit rough and ready for the casual visitor, and it's not exactly a welcoming place. Though we had a whole bunch of visitors just recently, who seemed as interested in the wood as the town. Some people here thought they might be checking out locations for a documentary, maybe even a television series. The town really liked the sound of that; they could smell serious money in the offing. But the newcomers turned out to be typical soulless media types, with no real appreciation of the town or its history. Vincent wouldn't have anything to do with them, and after a few unfortunate close encounters, neither would I. Awful people.'

'Do you think the thing in the sky was a UFO?' said Penny.

Frank's smile broadened, and his eyes sparkled. 'There are those who say there's no impact site or crater because the UFO just landed quietly and then took off again.' He gestured grandly at the *X-Files* poster. 'Facts are fun, but there's nothing to beat a good story. So, when in doubt, repeat the legend!

'Of all the oddities associated with this town, Vincent always seemed most fascinated by the UFO. Perhaps because it was so elusive. He was never happier than when he found an excuse to go tramping through the wood or the fields outside of town, following up on a new lead . . . but none of it ever came to anything.'

'Do you think it might have been a UFO?' Penny insisted.

'I like to think so,' said Frank. 'But then, I like to believe in all manner of things that probably aren't true, just because they make the world so much more interesting. Like the Loch Ness monster. If you sat me down in a court of law, under oath, I'd have no choice but to say there isn't enough evidence to justify its existence. But I like the idea of it being there.

'And it's probably safer for Nessie if she stays a legend. If she ever did stick her head above the water during some live television broadcast, so the whole world could see her, how long do you think it would be before some professional hunter turned up to try and shoot her? Or, worse still, some well-meaning scientists, determined to drag her out of the loch and carry her off to some special reserve, for her own good? No . . . she's better off as a myth.'

'Why do you think the story about the UFO persists after so long?' asked Penny.

'Because there's so little to it, people can put their own stamp on it, I suppose,' said Frank. 'Even after all these years, it's still bringing people like you here.'

I gestured at the *X-Files* poster. 'From what I remember of that show, not all the stories about alien encounters were happy ones.'

Frank nodded. 'Vincent used to say the same thing. He had a bee in his bonnet about the victims of alien abductions, and the awful things that were supposed to have happened to them. He kept saying he was going to write a book on the subject. He was obsessed with how stories about alien contact had changed down the decades. If you look at the earliest versions, they were all about beneficent space gods, come to Earth to dispense cosmic wisdom, but at some point, the aliens

became monsters, doing monstrous things. Vincent said, if
their stories are true, then these people have been through the
most horrific experience of their lives, but when they try to
explain what happened to them, they just get disbelieved and
laughed at. He thought that was adding insult to injury.'

'Why didn't he write the book?' I said.

'Because there have never been any such incidents around
here,' said Frank. 'He would have had to travel to the kind of
places where they did happen, so he could talk to the people
directly . . . And Vincent never wanted to leave the town.'

The phone at the main desk rang, and Frank excused himself
to go and answer it.

Penny looked at me.

'What do you know about alien abductions?'

'I've read about them,' I said. 'But I have no personal
knowledge in that area, and I've never met anyone who has.'

'What about all the conspiracy theories?' said Penny.
'That the governments of this world made a deal, allowing
aliens to take a certain number of people in return for
advanced technology?'

'No,' I said firmly. 'If anything like that was going on, I
would have heard about it. Black Heir was created to loot
crashed alien ships, because that's the only way to get alien
tech.'

Frank came back, and we rose to our feet as he smiled
easily at us. 'That was Ellie, making sure you got here safely.
And ordering me to tell you all the really juicy stories, so
you'd be sure to stay on at her hotel while you check them
out. She always was a mercenary soul . . . Now, where were
we, my cosmic children?'

'When, exactly, did this meteor appear over Norton
Hedley?' said Penny.

'In the early hours of the morning, on the fifth of August
1963,' said Frank.

Penny shot me a look, saying, *At least now we know when
your birthday is.*

'What is it that intrigues you about this particular UFO
sighting?' said Frank. 'There are better stories, in more acces-
sible places. Why come here?'

'Penny and I like to track down the stories no one else is looking at,' I said. 'In the hope we can turn up something that everyone else has missed.'

Frank smiled his gentle smile. 'I thought you looked the type. It's such a shame you missed Vincent. He would have loved talking to you.'

'That's what I had hoped,' I said.

'But after all these stories, and all the local history and folklore,' said Penny, 'what do you believe in, Frank? Have you ever seen anything out of the ordinary in Norton Hedley?'

Frank shook his head sadly. 'Not one single thing. And not for want of trying. I've walked up and down this town my whole life, and spent entire nights sitting out in the wood with a thermos and a torch, and never saw or felt anything. That's why I study all this stuff. Because it's the next best thing to being there. But I can sense you're keen to be on your way, so . . . Is there anything else I can help you with?'

'There is one thing,' I said. 'What is that huge mansion house that towers over the library? It seems so out of place, in the middle of town.'

Frank looked at me as though I'd slapped him. 'There's no mansion house here. Show me.'

He hurried us back through the library and out of the front door, and when we turned to look, there was no sign of a mansion house anywhere. The library stood alone, in a quiet little cul-de-sac, surrounded by nothing more than the usual period cottages. Frank shook his head slowly.

'You have seen Murdstone Manse – the ghost house that comes and goes, popping up here and there, all over the town. I am so jealous. I've lived here my whole life and never once caught a glimpse of it. Oh, well . . . that's life, in Norton Hedley.'

SIX

Not out of the Woods Yet

'You know,' said Frank, 'you really should consider taking a constitutional through the wood outside town.'

'I thought you said it was just trees?' said Penny.

'Oh, it is,' said Frank. 'But they're very atmospheric trees.'

He gave us one last glimpse of his gentle smile and then went back inside and shut the door, leaving Penny and me to look at where Murdstone Manse had stood.

'A ghost house?' said Penny. 'Really?'

'It looked very real,' I said. 'Right up to the point when it suddenly wasn't there any more.'

'I suppose it could have been some kind of timeslip . . .'

'Except that Murdstone Manse was supposed to have been situated somewhere on the edge of town, before it was burned down. Frank did seem to be suggesting that it could appear wherever it wanted.'

'Well, that's just weird,' said Penny.

'I wouldn't argue with that.'

'I think I'm taking this very well,' said Penny. 'Considering that a whole freaking mansion house just disappeared out from under us.'

'To be fair,' I said, 'it did have the good manners to wait until we weren't actually looking. But, yes . . . I'm freaking out, too – just a bit.'

'Only a bit?'

'Maybe I'm getting used to being in Norton Hedley.'

'Either that or it's some kind of supernatural culture shock.' Penny raised her chin and squared her shoulders. 'Come on; we can handle anything the town can throw at us. We're professionals. Where should we go next?'

'I would like to see Vincent Smith's cottage,' I said. 'But I think we should give Lucy enough time to do a thorough job.'

Penny grinned. 'A little of her unbridled enthusiasm does go a long way, doesn't it?'

'Not that I'm admitting anything,' I said, 'but perhaps we could kill some time with a stroll through the wood.'

'Any particular reason?'

'Because Frank made such a point of suggesting it. He didn't advise us to check out any other part of town, did he?'

Penny frowned. 'He went out of his way to assure us there was nothing weird about the wood, so why send us there?'

'Presumably because there is something there that he thinks we need to see.'

Penny reached resignedly for her phone. 'Give me a minute; I'll find us the quickest route.'

'No need,' I said. 'According to the research I did before we left London, the wood is so big it borders half the town. All we have to do is walk in a straight line until we run out of streets and then look around.'

'Does this wood have a suitably ominous name?' said Penny.

'No. I suppose when it's this close to the town, everyone knows which wood you mean.'

The afternoon was almost over, and the sun was sliding down the sky. Shadows lengthened as the light went out of the day. The streets were as empty as ever, but I was getting used to that. I strode briskly along, wondering what Frank thought the wood had to offer that could possibly top a disappearing mansion house. And whether it might have anything to do with all the people who'd vanished.

'You're frowning,' Penny said accusingly. 'Why are you frowning, darling? You'll get lines.'

'This town is bubbling over with all kinds of weird happenings,' I said. 'But it's the mystery of the missing people that stands out for me. So many of them, and apparently never a clue as to what might have happened.'

'Could the disappearances be connected to your ship?' said Penny. 'Some kind of alien abduction thing?'

'No,' I said patiently. 'People were going missing around here for centuries before my ship arrived.'

'You were the one who said we shouldn't get distracted

from the real reason we came here,' said Penny. 'We know your ship didn't crash in the wood because you saw it burying itself in the field.'

'I might have been wrong about that,' I said.

Penny looked at me searchingly. 'How can you be wrong? I mean, you saw it happen. Didn't you?'

'I'm not sure how much I trust my earliest memories,' I said. 'Not now I'm here. It's all so different from what I was expecting. Perhaps what I saw my ship doing is just a false memory, put in place by the transformation machines.'

'Why would they do that?' said Penny.

'To hide the truth from me,' I said.

'Why would they want to?'

'Perhaps for the same reason they concealed Vincent Smith's existence,' I said. 'Everything here seems to be hiding something . . .'

'I could check the exact number of disappearances on my phone,' said Penny. 'Then compare it to the town's population, and see if we can get some idea of the scale involved.'

'Go for it.'

Penny logged on and then made a series of increasingly annoyed noises. 'There's no mention of the missing people anywhere,' she said finally. 'Not even in the FAQ section. Frank did say the townspeople don't like to talk about it.'

'Understandable,' I said. 'You can't expect to attract tourists to a town where people just suddenly vanish.'

Penny put her phone away. 'What do you think this means?'

'It means Norton Hedley isn't just another small country town,' I said.

We kept walking until suddenly we ran out of streets. Civilization just stopped, as a line of old terraced houses butted up against the wood. Houses on one side of the street, trees on the other, with only the width of a road to separate them. The wood pressed right up to the edge of town and then stopped abruptly, as though only the presence of the houses kept it from advancing any further.

Penny and I came to a halt and studied the wood suspiciously. There was nothing about it to indicate why Frank had sent us here. The trees seemed normal enough, basking in the late-afternoon sunshine, their branches heavy with greenery. A gusting breeze carried all the scents of nature to me, along with the reassuring chirp and chatter of birdsong. A beaten trail stretched invitingly away before us, heading off into the heart of the wood. Just the spot to stretch your legs, it seemed to say, and enjoy the charms of an old English wood on a pleasant afternoon in autumn.

So why didn't I believe any of that? Penny moved in close beside me.

'Ishmael? What's wrong? You look like you're thinking of carpet-bombing the wood with Agent Orange.'

'Something about this doesn't feel right.'

Penny shrugged. 'Like the man said: it's just trees.'

'Then why make such a fuss?' I said. 'Frank did everything but give us a map and a guidebook, and a good push in the back to get us moving.'

'You think the trees are hiding something?' said Penny.

'Why should the wood be any different from the town?' I said. 'Nothing about Norton Hedley is what it seems.'

'Frank seemed straightforward enough,' said Penny. 'In a cosmic and groovy kind of way. I liked him.'

'Yes,' I said. 'He was very likeable. But you can't con someone unless you win their trust first.'

'It's just a wood!' said Penny.

'I don't think anything is just anything, in this town.'

'Are we going in or not?'

'I'm thinking about it.'

'We don't have to go in there if you don't want to,' said Penny. 'If you think it might be dangerous . . .'

I gave her a look, and she grinned at me. She always did know how to push my buttons.

'All the more reason to go in,' I said. 'If something is trying to hide from me, I want to know what it is. If only so it can't sneak up on me. And when I find whatever it is, I fully intend to wrestle it to the ground, kneel on its chest and ask it a whole bunch of really pertinent questions.'

'You do that,' said Penny. 'I'll stand well back and take notes.'

I looked at the path before us. Hard-beaten earth, with a scattering of leaves; a simple open trail with no obvious obstacles or pitfalls. Nothing in the least bit suspicious about it. Except that all it lacked was a big neon sign saying *This Way to the Gingerbread Cottage*. I couldn't resist a quick smile.

'What?' said Penny.

'If something is so determined to lure us in, it would be rude not to accept their invitation,' I said.

Penny grinned. 'Because you never met a trap you didn't like.'

'I never met a trap I couldn't beat into submission with both arms tied behind my back,' I said cheerfully.

'I don't think even you can out-wrestle a bunch of trees,' said Penny.

'It wooden be difficult,' I said solemnly. 'Leaf it to me.'

'Do you want a slap?' said Penny. 'Only I've got one, right here in my pocket.'

I laughed and plunged into the open trail, with Penny right there at my side.

And everything changed.

The autumnal sunlight disappeared in a moment, replaced by a deep foreboding gloom. The tall trees were suddenly stark, leafless shapes, packed close together, with deep dark shadows in between. Like the trees I'd seen earlier, on the edge of the field. The trail was gone too, and the dark earth floor looked treacherously uneven. The air was still and unseasonably cold, with not even a hint of birdsong.

'All right,' Penny said steadily, 'what just happened?'

'The wood isn't pretending any more,' I said. 'This is its true face.'

'Do you think Frank knew about this?'

'He must have known something.'

I looked behind us, and the gap we'd used to enter the wood was gone as well. All I could see was more trees, fading away into the gloom.

'The town can't just have vanished!' said Penny.

'Norton Hedley is famous for its disappearances,' I said.

'But we just came in that way!' said Penny. And then she stopped and peered uncertainly about her. 'Didn't we? I feel a bit . . . turned around. As though I've lost all sense of direction.'

'I think we've lost more than that,' I said. 'I'm not even sure what time of day it is.'

Penny nodded quickly. 'I can't tell whether it's day or night. It feels like we've been set adrift in time.'

'Cut loose from the world,' I said.

'As traps go, this one gets a gold ribbon and a mention in dispatches,' Penny said steadily. 'How are we going to get out of here, Ishmael?'

'Walk forward in a straight line,' I said. 'The wood isn't that big; if we just keep going, we're bound to come out the other side.'

'It must be wonderful to be so confident all the time.'

'Oh, it is,' I said. 'You have no idea.'

Penny slipped an arm through mine, probably just to steady herself on the uneven ground, and we moved forward together.

'This reminds me of the deep dark woods in all the old fairy tales,' Penny said quietly. 'Usually on the way to Granny's cottage, to find out that the wolf has already eaten her.'

'I always thought that was really a werewolf story,' I said.

'You would.'

We pressed on, occasionally stumbling over exposed roots that had burst up out of the broken ground, as though trying to escape. I carefully avoided the gnarled branches that reached out like clutching hands, and strained my eyes against the deepening gloom. Normally, my more-than-human eyes allow me to see clearly no matter how dark it gets, but there was something in this darkness that didn't want to be seen.

'Frank was right when he said the wood had an atmosphere,' said Penny, her voice entirely steady. 'Though why he thought we'd enjoy this . . .'

'I don't actually recall him using that word,' I said.

'He kept saying it was just trees,' said Penny. 'But it's so quiet and still . . . No birds singing, no buzz of insects . . . no wildlife anywhere. What kind of self-respecting wood doesn't have at least a few squirrels in it?'

'We are seeing the wood out of season,' I said. 'No doubt it puts on a much better show in the summer.'

'It must do,' said Penny. 'I can't see your average tourist spending five minutes in this before freaking out and running for his life. And yet . . . I'm sure Frank said there were photos and films, proving this was all trees.'

'Maybe this is just the bad part of the wood,' I said. 'And the rest of it is quite pleasant.'

'Well, find me the pleasant part and I'll go there.' She shivered suddenly. 'I swear it's getting colder. Why is it so cold in here?'

'Look up,' I said.

The trees were leaning over us, their branches interlocking to form a heavy canopy – keeping the light out and holding darkness within. There were a few gaps, where light from outside fell through like spotlights on a deserted stage. They didn't illuminate much, and their light was cold and grey, as though the sun had nothing to do with them.

'It's like someone's putting on a show,' I said.

'Then where's the audience?' said Penny.

The wood was getting darker, the shadows deeper. The trees were crammed in so close now that Penny and I had to walk in single file to get past them. Up close, the wrinkled bark on the tree trunks looked like screaming faces. Gnarled branches seemed to twitch and clutch on the edge of my vision, although they were always still when I turned to look at them. The dirt floor had disappeared beneath a thick mulch of decaying leaves that slipped and slid under our feet. The air was heavy with the smell of dead things.

'This is starting to feel more like the woods in the older, darker fairy tales,' Penny said quietly. 'Not the cleaned-up editions they let children read, but the original savage versions, red in tooth and claw. Where the monsters triumph and the wolf eats the young heroine. Sometimes, he does other things to her. This is like every bad dream I ever had, growing up.'

'I never had a lot of time for fairy stories,' I said. 'But then, I never had a childhood. What did the young heroines usually do to survive?'

'Left a trail of breadcrumbs, or depended on the kindness of passing woodsmen with really sharp axes.'

'If a big bad wolf does show up, I'll make a coat out of him for you,' I said.

And then I came to a sudden halt as I saw something familiar looming up ahead of us. It was the old mansion house, Murdstone Manse, standing alone in the middle of the wood. The trees came right up to its walls, and the branches clattered against the windows as though trying to force their way in. The gabled roof disappeared into the overhead canopy. The old house looked as though it had always been there, and the wood had grown up around it. And then all of the windows were suddenly full of light, blazing so brightly I had to turn my face away. When I was able to look again, the house was gone.

Penny gripped my arm with both hands. 'Ishmael? What the hell just happened?'

'It was the mansion house,' I said.

'I know that! But what was it doing here?'

'Maybe it followed us,' I said.

'Why would it do that?'

'Why do ghost houses do anything?' I said.

'It must mean something,' said Penny. 'Maybe this is what Frank wanted us to see.'

I started to answer and then broke off and looked around.

'What?' said Penny.

'We've been walking through this wood for some time,' I said slowly. 'So why haven't we reached the other side?'

No matter which way I looked, all I could see were trees and the shadows between the trees, deep and dark like patches of night.

'How long have we been walking?' said Penny. She brought her wrist up to her face so she could study the glowing dial. 'Ishmael, my watch has stopped.'

I didn't even bother to look at mine. I thought we'd been walking in a straight line, but with no path and a complete lack of landmarks . . .

'Is it just me,' Penny said quietly, 'or is the wood getting darker?'

'It's not just you.'

'Damn,' said Penny. 'I was really hoping it was me.'

'It feels as though we're surrounded,' I said. 'And, just possibly, as if we're being herded somewhere.'

'Wherever that is, we don't want to go there,' Penny said immediately. 'Maybe we should start breaking some branches off the trees.'

I looked at her. 'What good would that do?'

'It would show we mean business. That we're prepared to defend ourselves.'

'Against what?' I said. 'All I see is trees, and they don't look like they're getting ready to jump us and drag us down.'

'Are you sure about that?' said Penny. 'Doesn't it feel to you as if they're moving closer together, to make sure we never get out?'

'Trees don't do that,' I said.

'Not in any normal forest, but we've come a long way from normal.' And then she stopped, as an idea struck her. 'Ishmael . . . you said your ship buried itself deep in the earth. Could there have been – I don't know . . . radiation, chemical spills, that leaked out of the broken ship and into the ground, and got soaked up by the tree roots? Could your ship have changed the nature of this wood into something else? Something alien?'

'None of this looks familiar to me,' I said.

'When we found that computer under the house on Widows Hill, you spoke to it and it obeyed you,' said Penny, 'because it was your people's technology. If this wood was made by your ship . . .'

'This doesn't feel like my people's work,' I said. 'Far more likely that this is the town's influence. We have no idea how far the town's weird stuff travels.'

'Maybe this is where people go missing,' said Penny. 'They come into the wood and then find they can't get out again.'

'Then where are all the bodies?' I said.

'In the ground,' said Penny. 'Taken up by the roots and the trees.'

I looked at her. 'Man-eating trees? Is that really what you're going with?'

Penny scowled around her. 'I keep getting the feeling that something's moving, deep in the shadows . . .'

'There's no one else in the wood,' I said. 'I'd know. It's just us and the trees.'

'Ishmael . . . look at the trees up ahead. They're moving.'

'The branches aren't even stirring from a passing breeze – because there isn't one,' I said steadily. 'Don't let your imagination get the better of you.'

'Ishmael,' said Penny, 'I am seeing what I'm seeing.'

I nodded. 'I believe you. What do you want me to do?'

'Either you come up with a really good idea to get us out of this, or I am going back to my ripping-off-branches idea. Even if I have to dismantle every single tree between us and the way out.'

I thought for a moment and then raised my voice to address the wood.

'Everywhere I look, all I see is firewood. So either you show us a way out, right now, or I am going to use my lighter to burn down everything that stands between us and the outside world.'

There was a pause, and then Penny's grip tightened on my arm. 'Ishmael! Is that a path?'

'It'll do,' I said.

We hurried along the new trail, and a few moments later we were outside the wood and blinking dazedly in bright daylight, facing perfectly normal streets and houses. I looked behind me, and the trees were all standing a sane and safe distance apart, bathed in autumn sun. Birds were singing happily, and what shadows remained were only shadows.

'Well,' said Penny, sounding perfectly composed, 'that was interesting. What the hell was it, Ishmael?'

'It would appear that there's more to that wood than meets the mind,' I said.

'You think what we experienced was only in our heads?' said Penny.

'Wouldn't surprise me,' I said.

'So we were never in any real danger?'

'I wouldn't go that far,' I said. 'Do you want to go back in there and check?'

'I wouldn't go back in there without a chainsaw in both hands,' said Penny. She looked at me. 'Would you really have set fire to the wood, with us in it?'

'That might have proved a bit difficult,' I said, 'given that I don't actually own a lighter.'

We laughed quietly together, turned away from the wood and headed back into town.

'At least now we know there's more to the town than just stories,' said Penny. 'Some of the weird stuff is real.'

'Maybe that's what Frank wanted us to learn,' I said.

Penny sniffed loudly. 'I would have been perfectly happy to take his word for it. Where are we going now?'

'Back to the hotel,' I said. 'And our nice little room on the top floor. We could use a time out and a chance to do some hard thinking. I had a plan all worked out for what I was going to do once I'd had a chance to talk to Vincent Smith . . . But since he might be dead, and Mr Almond definitely is, that changes everything. It would appear Norton Hedley has its own secrets, which may or may not be connected to why we're here. At the very least, it would seem we're stuck in another murder mystery. We need to find out who killed whom, and why – if only to establish whether or not it's anything to do with us.'

'And if it isn't?' said Penny. 'This isn't what we came here for, Ishmael. We don't know what we're getting into. It might be better to just walk away and leave this town to its own problems.'

'No,' I said. 'I need to know what's going on here.'

'You always do,' said Penny.

SEVEN

Violet Silver Investigates

We headed back to the Pale Horse, both of us lost in our own thoughts. I was looking forward to a nice lie down and a bit of a time out while, from the way she was walking, Penny couldn't wait to get her shoes off. But we'd only just passed through the front door when Ellie Markham's voice blasted across the lobby like a lighthouse foghorn warning of imminent collisions and sea monsters rising from the depths.

'Mr Jones! Ms Belcourt!'

My first impulse was to just keep walking and pretend I hadn't heard anything, but Ellie was already bustling forward to block our way, positively bristling with excitement and self-importance.

'Oh, I am pleased to see you again, dears! You won't believe what's happened!'

'We were just going up to our room,' I said, but Ellie planted herself firmly in front of us, bursting with important news she was determined to share, even if she had to wrestle us to the ground and shout it into our faces.

'There's someone here to talk to you, dears,' she said. 'She's been waiting for ages. I did phone Frank at the library so he could tell you, but you'd already left. Where have you been all this time?'

'We went for a walk in the wood,' said Penny.

'Rather you than me, dears,' said Ellie. 'I wouldn't go in there for all the teabags in China. I've never been one for nature. It's always so messy . . .'

'Who is it that wants to see us?' I said, dragging us back to the matter at hand.

'And why is it so important?' said Penny.

'Hasn't anyone told you?' said Ellie. 'It's all over the

town! Winston Almond, the town undertaker, has been found dead. In the town mortuary! The police are saying it could be murder!'

She sounded more pleased than shocked, as though already calculating just how much tourist money there was to be made from a good local murder.

'The undertaker?' I said, being careful to sound a little confused as well as surprised. 'How did he die?'

'They're saying he just dropped dead!' said Ellie. 'But Winston wasn't even my age, and he was in perfect health. He did jogging and everything.'

'What was he doing in the mortuary?' said Penny.

Ellie leaned in close and lowered her voice confidentially, even though we were the only ones in the lobby.

'Apparently, Vincent didn't have any family that anyone knows of, so Frank contacted Winston and said he'd pay for the funeral. As long as it was kept simple and basic.' Ellie smirked knowingly. 'He meant cheap. So it seems Winston said he'd go in on his lunch break and measure the body, just to get things started. And now – you won't believe this, but it's true – Vincent's body has disappeared! No one knows what's happened to it!'

'Why would anyone want to talk to us about that?' I said, though I was pretty sure I already knew the answer.

'It's the police!' Ellie said importantly. 'The inspector is waiting for you in the snug.'

'But we're just tourists,' said Penny. 'We only arrived here today.'

'Oh, I'm sure she's talking to everyone, dear,' said Ellie.

'We don't know anything,' I said.

'I don't think anyone does,' said Ellie. 'Or the inspector would be out chasing after them, instead of propping up my bar. Normally, she wouldn't be caught dead in there, if you'll pardon the expression. You'd better go on through, dears. The inspector can get very shirty if she's kept waiting. She was just the same when we were at school. I told her she could help herself to anything she fancied from behind the bar, as long as she left the money by the till, but I doubt even that's going to be enough to put her in a good mood.'

I nodded resignedly. 'Keep our room warm. We won't be long.'

Penny and I slipped past Ellie on both sides at once and headed for the adjoining bar, taking our time, without being too obvious about it.

'I wasn't expecting Almond's body to be discovered so quickly,' I said quietly to Penny. 'Someone must have checked the mortuary right after we left.'

'Perhaps that's why the hospital put on that show – to hold our attention,' said Penny. 'So someone could rush round to the mortuary and see what we did there.' She scowled at the entrance to the bar. 'Why is this inspector so determined to talk to us?'

'Because we're outsiders, I suppose.'

'Do you think she knows we came here looking for Vincent Smith?' said Penny.

'Wouldn't surprise me,' I said. 'In a town this small, everyone always knows everyone else's business. But remember: we don't know anything about anything.'

'Oh, please,' said Penny. 'Like we haven't danced this dance before.'

The only person in the hotel snug was a large middle-aged woman perched awkwardly on a bar stool, wearing what looked like gardening clothes. She had a mannish face, neatly trimmed grey hair, and a dumpy figure that wasn't exactly flattered by the baggy clothes. She hadn't helped herself to a drink, but she was making short work of a large bag of peanuts. She pretended not to notice when we entered the bar, and waited till we were almost upon her before she turned unhurriedly to face us. She started to say something, and then stopped and smiled apologetically as she emptied her mouth first. A nicely self-deprecating moment, to put us at our ease in the presence of an authority figure. I felt like applauding. When she was done, she looked us over with eyes so sleepy as to seem almost disinterested. It was a good look for a professional and would probably have fooled anyone else.

'Mr Ishmael Jones and Ms Penny Belcourt?' she said, in a carefully disarming mild and pleasant voice. 'So good to meet you at last. Sorry to interrupt your little holiday; I'll do my best not to detain you too long. I'm Detective Inspector Violet Silver. Do call me Violet. No need to make this any more formal than it needs to be. I hope you don't mind, but I'm afraid I need to ask you a few questions. There's been a murder, you see, right here in Norton Hedley.'

'Of course,' I said. 'Anything we can do to help. But we're just tourists. We only got into town this afternoon.'

'So we don't know anything about Mr Almond's death,' said Penny.

'Now that's interesting,' said Violet. 'How on earth do you know the name of the dead man, Ms Belcourt? I'm sure I hadn't got around to mentioning that yet.'

'Ellie told us as we came in,' I said. 'She was just brimming over with the news.'

'Of course she was,' said Violet. 'That woman couldn't keep her mouth shut if you stapled her lips together. She was just the same at school.'

Her voice and her gaze were suddenly a lot sharper, but I made a point of not noticing.

'I can't believe we've only been in town for a few hours, and already someone has been murdered!' said Penny. She was using her best *gosh and golly* voice, complete with wide eyes. 'It's so exciting! Of course, it's terrible, too.'

'Especially for me,' said Violet, sounding almost terminally sleepy and detached again. 'This was supposed to be my day off. I was right in the middle of some important weeding when the call came. You have to keep on top of weeds or they'll eat your garden alive. But since I live right here in the town, it's been given to me to deal with the first actual homicide in Norton Hedley since 1928.'

'Who was killed then?' I asked politely.

'No one you'd know,' said Violet. 'I've been promised backup, but God alone knows when they'll get here, so for now it's just me. Shall we get started? Good, good . . . that's the ticket. When exactly did the two of you turn up here?'

I gave her all the details, and she pretended she didn't already know them. I had no doubt that no-need-to-call-me-Inspector Violet was the kind who always did her homework, and probably handed it in early, too. She listened carefully, nodding along and making interested noises. I explained how Penny and I had come to Norton Hedley to investigate the town's UFO story, and when I was done, she smiled easily.

'I thought you looked the type – all enthusiastic and dedicated. What parts of town have you been looking at?'

I ran her through our day, keeping the timing as vague as possible, in case I might need some wiggle room later on.

'Have you been anywhere near the hospital?' said Violet.

'I don't know,' I said. 'Where is it?'

Violet didn't apologize for such an obvious trap; just looked even sleepier as she moved on to the next line of attack.

'Ellie said you went to talk to Frank Kendall at the library, but when she phoned, you weren't there . . .'

'We'd already left,' I said.

'And what did you talk to Frank about?'

'We're big fans of Vincent Smith's books,' said Penny. 'Especially the one about the UFO. Ellie told us Frank was the man to talk to, when it came to the weird stuff.'

I nodded happily in agreement. 'He had a lot of interesting things to say about the stranger aspects of the town. We already knew some of it, of course, from reading Mr Smith's books. Did you know him?'

'Oh, yes,' said Violet. 'I knew him. Where did you go after you left the library?'

'We took a nice stroll through the wood,' I said. 'Frank said we'd find it very atmospheric.'

'And it was,' said Penny. 'Very.'

'I suppose so,' Violet said kindly. 'If you're a tourist.'

'Frank told us there were all kinds of fascinating stories attached to the wood,' I said, just a bit reproachfully.

'There isn't a part of this town that isn't linked to one wild story or another,' said Violet. 'But I wouldn't have thought the wood had anything to do with the UFO?'

'It was supposed to have landed somewhere around there,' I said, showing just the right amount of hope and enthusiasm.

'But we walked all the way through the wood and didn't see anything out of the ordinary,' said Penny, with an admirably straight face.

'You shouldn't believe everything Frank tells you,' said Violet.

'Bu he's a librarian!' said Penny, sounding honestly shocked.

I nodded quickly. 'He had a lot to say about the mysterious disappearances here in Norton Hedley.'

Violet shrugged. 'The numbers are a bit high for the area. But it's nothing to worry about. Just a statistical anomaly.'

'Who was the last local person to disappear?' I said.

'That would be Vincent Smith,' said Violet. 'Or, at least, his body. Which isn't in the mortuary, where it should be.'

'Yes, we know,' Penny said blithely.

Violet shot her a sharp look, started to lean forward on her stool and then stopped herself.

'Ellie told you, didn't she?'

'According to her, the story is all over the town,' I said. 'I have to say, it sounds a bit odd to me. How can a body go missing without anyone noticing? Doesn't the hospital have any security?'

'Not so you'd notice,' Violet said dryly. 'But he's definitely not there. Trust me. We looked everywhere.'

'We travelled halfway across the country to talk to Mr Smith,' I said, 'only to find he'd died just before we got here. Bit of a shock, that.'

'But we weren't going to let it spoil our holiday,' Penny said stoutly. 'Not after we'd come so far.'

'Of course,' said Violet. She fixed me with a thoughtful look. 'Now, you wanted to talk to Mr Smith because . . .'

'Because of the book he wrote about the UFO,' I said.

'Why are you so interested in this particular sighting?' said Violet.

'Because we'd never heard of it,' I said. 'And we thought we knew all the UFO stories.'

'Do you know anything about it?' Penny said hopefully, still doing the wide-eyed bit.

'That was all well before my time,' said Violet. 'And not really my line of work.' She sat back on her stool and studied us thoughtfully with her heavy-lidded eyes, waiting for us to volunteer something useful. When that didn't happen, she nodded slowly, as though she hadn't expected it to be that easy. 'Will you be staying on in town, now that the man you came to see is no longer with us?'

'We'll hang around a few days, I think,' I said. 'See if there's anything else we might want to take an interest in. Frank made it sound as though there's a lot of weird stuff going on here.'

Violet smiled and shrugged, as though none of this was in any way important. 'Frank always did spend too much time inside his own head.'

'What's the official police position on all these mysteries?' Penny said brightly.

'Unless someone is breaking the law, it's nothing to do with us,' said Violet.

'This Mr Almond . . .' I said. 'You are sure he was murdered? It couldn't have been some kind of accident? You didn't say how he died.'

'You're right, Mr Jones, I didn't,' said Violet. 'The cause of death has yet to be established. But the circumstances are suspicious; the door to the mortuary was always kept locked, but somebody broke in.'

I just nodded. Violet waited a moment to see if I had anything more to say, but I just stared calmly back at her.

'I hate to be a nuisance,' Violet said easily, 'but I'm going to have to ask you to show me some form of ID.'

'Of course,' I said.

I got out my driving licence, and she carefully jotted down all the details in her notebook. While she was doing that, I caught Penny's eye and shook my head slightly. So that when Violet returned my licence and turned to Penny, she said all her things were upstairs in our room. Violet looked as if she wanted to tell Penny to run upstairs and get some ID, but she didn't.

'Not to worry,' she said. 'I have all of Mr Jones's details. And now, if you'll excuse me, I have to be about my business.'

'Aren't you going to tell us not to leave town?' I said hopefully.

'They always say that in the television shows,' said Penny.

'Someone will let me know if you try,' said Violet.

She slid down from her bar stool, stuffed the bag of peanuts into her pocket and then ambled drowsily out of the bar. I watched her carefully, just in case she was planning to try a Columbo and suddenly turn around with a *Just one last question* . . . But that didn't happen. I watched the door close behind her, and when I'd allowed enough time to be sure she was out of earshot, I turned to Penny.

'All the local cops we could have got, and we had to get a smart one.'

'You think she suspects us?' said Penny.

'She'd be a fool if she didn't,' I said. 'We are the only outsiders in town.'

'What are we going to do, now that Vincent Smith is dead?' said Penny. 'There's no one else who can give us the answers we were hoping for.'

'The truth is still out there,' I said solemnly.

We gave Violet enough time to leave, and then a bit more, just in case she was lurking in the lobby. I peered cautiously out of the snug door to make sure the coast was clear, and then we launched ourselves out of the bar and headed for the front door. Ellie immediately called after us.

'Mr Jones, Ms Belcourt! Aren't you going up to your room after all, dears? I've changed the sheets and everything.'

We didn't slow down or even look back. We didn't want to get trapped in another endless conversation.

'We're just going out into the town, to see what's happening,' I said.

'It's all so exciting!' said Penny.

And then we were out of the door and gone, before Ellie could come up with any reason to stop us leaving.

'So now we have a deadline,' I said as we hurried down the street. 'We need to get to the truth of what's going on here before Violet checks my ID and the police computers laugh in her face.'

Penny looked at me sharply. 'I thought the Organization provided you with ID that would fool anyone?'

'They do,' I said. 'But I couldn't use that one, because we're not here officially. What I showed the inspector was just one of my many unofficial backup IDs.'

'How many do you have?' said Penny.

'As many as I need.'

Penny looked at me admiringly. 'You don't even trust the Organization, do you?'

'I don't trust anyone,' I said. 'Except you, of course.'

'Nice save, darling. But why not contact the Colonel and make this an official investigation? Then the inspector would have to leave us alone.'

'I can't do that without explaining to the Organization why I'm here,' I said. 'So, first rule of a mystery: when you're in a hole, keep digging, to see what you can uncover.'

'I should have known this would turn out to be a working holiday,' said Penny. 'Where are we going first?'

'Vincent Smith's cottage,' I said. 'I want to see what Lucy has turned up.'

EIGHT
Hidden in Plain Sight

We hurried along the street, putting the Pale Horse behind us as quickly as we could. I was at least half convinced that Ellie might come running out of the hotel and chase after us, so she could talk at us some more. Penny got out her phone to check the town website again.

'If you're looking for Vincent Smith's address, I already know it,' I said. 'It was in the Organization report.'

Penny looked at me. 'You remember his address? Just from reading it once?'

'Of course,' I said.

'Alien,' said Penny.

She accessed the website map anyway, to work out the quickest way to Smith's cottage. We were both a little disturbed to discover it was out on the edge of town, right next to the wood.

'How was he able to stand living that close to something so creepy?' said Penny.

'Perhaps it didn't affect him,' I said. 'Like the people living in that row of terraced houses facing the trees.'

Penny shrugged. 'Live in a weird town long enough, I suppose it's inevitable that you're going to end up weird, too.'

'Good thing I was only passing through the first time,' I said.

'I don't know,' said Penny. 'It would explain a lot about you.'

I looked down my nose at her. 'I am not weird.'

'Of course not, darling. You're just differently normal. And that's a whole separate kettle of alien.'

'You are so supportive.'

'I try.'

We pressed on through the town, stepping out at a decent pace because we were both getting a little tired of Norton Hedley's streets. I was reminded of those old cartoon shows, where the characters keep moving but the background stays the same. We bumped into a few people along the way, and to my surprise they all nodded politely as we passed. No sign of a smile or so much as a word of greeting, but it was a start. Perhaps the townspeople were finally getting used to seeing us around. And yet, even after we'd left them behind and the streets were empty again, I couldn't shake off a feeling of being watched by unseen eyes. I looked around quickly, half hoping to catch someone or something by surprise.

'Are you getting that "We are not alone" feeling again?' Penny said patiently.

'I don't know,' I said. 'Maybe.'

'Is it the same feeling you had on the train, coming in?'

'I don't know. Maybe.'

'What do you think was going on in the wood?' said Penny, kindly changing the subject.

'Some form of genius loci,' I said. 'Something that affects the minds of everyone who passes through. If you go in expecting *just trees*, then that's what you'll see. Which is why tourists' photos and films never show anything out of the ordinary. Their cameras only record what's actually there. But other people . . . see other things.'

'Why did we get the full horror show?' said Penny. 'I wasn't expecting anything in particular.'

'That might have been down to me,' I said. 'Whatever was in that wood, or possibly underneath it, reacting to the non-human side of my nature.'

'Underneath? You mean the buried ship?'

'It might have been trying to scare us off, because it doesn't want to be found.'

Penny shook her head. 'You are so far past paranoia you can see it in your rear-view mirror.'

'Objects in the mirror can be closer than you think,' I said solemnly.

'Why do you think Frank made such a point of sending

us to the wood?' said Penny. 'Did he know it was going to mess with our minds?'

'He spent a lot of time talking with Vincent Smith,' I said. 'And who knows what that man might have known? Perhaps we'll find some clues at his cottage to help us understand what's going on.'

'We'd better,' Penny said darkly. 'I am getting really tired of walking back and forth in this town.'

I had enough sense not to glance at her fashionable shoes. Instead, I made a point of staring straight ahead, as though in search of inspiration.

'Vincent Smith first appeared in Norton Hedley in the sixties, as a young man,' I said. 'Maybe he chose a cottage on the edge of town because it's close to where the ship is buried.'

'According to Frank, though, Smith spent decades trying to discover the location of the crash site,' said Penny.

'It's always possible the transformation machines did a number on his memories, as well as mine,' I said. 'He knew there was a reason he had to live out on the edge; he just didn't know what it was. Perhaps he only recently discovered the ship, and that's what got him killed.'

'Who would want to kill him because of that?' said Penny.

'Some group who hoped to profit from the ship's tech,' I said. 'My people's enemies – to prevent him from escaping. Or perhaps the ship itself didn't want to be found, so it reached out and killed him.'

Penny shook her head. 'I thought we came here to find some answers, not more questions.'

'That's life,' I said. 'Or my life, anyway.'

'Mine too, now,' said Penny.

We shared a smile.

'I say we turn Smith's cottage upside down and shake it, and see what falls out,' I said. 'Maybe that will give us some idea of what we're dealing with.'

'You don't think he'll be there, do you?' said Penny.

I frowned. 'I can't see him being that stupid. It's the first place anyone would look. Far more likely he's on the run and in the wind.'

'But why would he fake his death in the first place?' said Penny. 'Frank was genuinely upset. I could tell.'

She was carefully not looking in my direction, but I knew she was talking about me as much as Smith. I was finally being forced to confront the truth: that I had behaved just as badly when I disappeared, to avoid being found out for what I was. I left good friends behind, who never knew what had happened to me.

'I always believed I was protecting my friends, as well as me,' I said, not looking at Penny. 'Because if I was under suspicion, they might be in danger, too. Just for knowing me. I couldn't even warn them, because they might have tried to stop me, and I couldn't afford to be stopped. I knew it would be hard on them, but I justified what I did by believing it was necessary. Now . . . I'm not so sure.'

Penny put her arm through mine. 'It's not too late. You could still track people down and contact them from a distance, without having to reveal where you are now.'

'No,' I said. 'I can't. My enemies could use my old friends to find me. Or hurt them, to get at me. I won't put them in danger.'

'But you have the Organization to hide you from the world!' said Penny.

'But what if I have to leave the Organization?' I said. 'They've been good to me, but I thought I was safe with other groups, before this. People at the top are always changing, and the ones you trust end up being replaced by new faces with different agendas. The more I do for people, the more they want to know how I did it.'

'Would it really be so bad if the world found out about you?' said Penny.

'Nothing scares a government more than the unknown,' I said steadily. 'I could end up dissected in a laboratory, or interrogated in some shadowy cellar for information on my ship and my people. Or they might just kill me, because what I represent is too much for them to cope with. Remember how you freaked out earlier at the idea of aliens moving among humanity, unseen and unsuspected?'

'Well,' said Penny, 'they don't know you like I do.'

We shared a smile.

'But mostly, I stay hidden because I don't know what kind of history my people have with Earth,' I said. 'The computer under the house on Widows Hill dated back to Victorian times, and there could have been other contacts before that. Why do my people keep coming back to Earth? It might be for good reasons, or bad, or something the human mind could never hope to understand. I know there's a war going on, out among the stars, but I have no idea what the stakes are, or what kind of allies both sides might have here on Earth.

'The only way for me to stay safe is to stay off the page and under everyone's radar. From aliens and humans and all the subterranean groups. I don't care about any of their agendas. All I've ever wanted is to live as a human, among humans.'

'Like Vincent Smith did,' said Penny.

'Yes,' I said. 'How did he survive here for so long with no protection? Because he never got personally involved with the weird stuff? When I used my abilities to serve those underground groups, was I actually drawing attention to myself?'

'Lucy did say we were legends,' Penny said dryly.

'I hate to think I spent so long serving unworthy masters, when I could have been living an ordinary life, like Vincent Smith.'

'But if you had, we'd never have met,' said Penny.

'Yes,' I said, smiling. 'There is that. For all his quiet existence here in Norton Hedley, it doesn't sound like Smith ever found anyone to share his life with. I don't envy him that.'

We walked on for a while, lost in our own thoughts.

'Do you think Smith is dead or alive?' Penny said finally.

'If he'd just disappeared, I'd say he was almost certainly still alive somewhere,' I said. 'But the dead undertaker complicates things. Someone must have killed him, and it's always possible Smith is another victim. But it wouldn't surprise me at all to discover that Smith set all of this up, to leave his enemies chasing shadows.'

'Would you do that to me?' Penny said bluntly. 'Just vanish, without warning, and never contact me again?'

'Of course not,' I said. *Unless that was the only way to protect you.*

*   *   *

There was no sudden edge to the town this time. Instead, the streets just seemed to wither away, in a series of increasingly separate picturesque houses. To get to Vincent Smith's place, we had to walk up a narrow lane that was little more than a dirt track, to stand before a small, single-storey cottage with walls that had probably started out as the usual creamy local stone, but now had a grey and grubby look. There were tiles missing from the roof, and the squat chimney stack lurched to one side. The whole place looked under siege, from time and the elements. But the walled garden that fronted the cottage looked pleasant enough, full of neatly tended shrubs and bees buzzing lazily around nodding flowers. There was a sundial, a bird table, and a set of hanging chimes that made soft ringing tones the moment I pushed open the gate. *Good early warning system*, I thought. And then I stopped and looked thoughtfully back the way we'd come.

'What is it now, Ishmael?' said Penny. 'If you frown any harder, you'll strain something.'

'There are no other houses,' I said. 'The nearest is back at the start of the lane. But Lucy said she was approached by one of Smith's neighbours to tell her he was dead. So where did this helpful neighbour come from?'

'Some passer-by?' said Penny.

'We're at the end of a lane,' I said. 'There's nowhere to pass by.'

'Maybe they were just curious as to who she was,' said Penny. 'Small town, remember?'

I looked at the field next to the cottage, stretching off into the distance and bordered on one side by the wood. The trees looked to be a reasonable distance apart, but the shadows within were very dark. I went back to looking at the cottage.

'You're still frowning,' said Penny. 'What's wrong?'

'Is this how he survived?' I said. 'By being so alone?'

'He had friends,' said Penny. 'Frank and Ellie . . .'

'But how much of his life could he share with them?' I said. 'Smith had the same enemies I do. Is that why he lived all the way out here, on the edge of town? So he would be able to see his enemies when they finally came for him?'

I stared at the cottage, and it stared right back at me, giving nothing away. The whole setting was doing its best to look charmingly innocent, and I wasn't buying any of it. Penny stirred impatiently.

'What exactly are we looking for, Ishmael?'

'Well, to start with, I'm wondering why Lucy hasn't noticed we've turned up and come running out to be enthusiastic at us.'

'Maybe she couldn't find anything and left.'

'Then why didn't she track us down to tell us that?' I said. 'Something isn't right here.'

'Well, we won't find out what it is by standing around here . . .'

I started up the path that led to the front door, and Penny slipped easily in beside me. The scent of late-summer flowers was heavy on the air, and the rich sunlight picked out all the colours in the garden. Anywhere else, I would have found it a very peaceful setting. But the house was just too still, and too quiet. As though it held secrets within.

'Do you think something might have happened to Lucy?' Penny said quietly.

'Something happened to Smith,' I said. 'And the undertaker.'

'And we sent her out here, on her own.'

'She's Black Heir. I thought she could look after herself.'

'Then where is she?'

'She could have gone missing,' I said. 'There's a lot of that going on around here.'

'Don't be flippant, Ishmael. If we sent her into danger—'

'She's Black Heir!'

'We should have come with her.'

I didn't say anything. Because Penny was right.

The front door was standing just a little ajar. I pushed it all the way open, hard enough that it slammed back against the inside wall. The impact echoed through the cottage, but there was no response. I listened hard but I couldn't hear anything. The house was silent as the grave. I stepped inside, slowly and cautiously, alert for anything unpleasant that might have been left behind for an unwary visitor.

Penny wanted to move in beside me, but the hall was too

narrow, so she settled for crowding in close and peering over my shoulder. The hall was decorated with old-fashioned flowery wallpaper and framed prints of old naval battles. The carpet had been there so long its pattern had been worn away. An old overcoat and a flat cap hung on the coat rack, as though their owner had just stepped out for a moment. The atmosphere was so still I could almost feel it pressing against me as I moved forward.

'Can you hear anything?' Penny said quietly.

'There's nothing moving anywhere in the house,' I said. 'But I really don't like the door being left open.'

'I just had a horrid thought,' Penny said slowly. 'What if Lucy is lying dead on the floor somewhere, like the undertaker?'

'There isn't a body here,' I said. 'I'd have smelled it by now.'

'Oh, ick,' said Penny. But her heart wasn't in it.

The first door leading off the hall turned out to be a bedroom, and one look told me all I needed to know. The bed had been stripped of its sheets and then overturned. The furniture had been thrown around, and everything delicate or ornamental had been smashed. Even the framed paintings from the walls had been torn down and strewn across the floor. Penny made a low shocked sound behind me.

'I know we told Lucy to be thorough, but . . .'

'I don't think this was her,' I said. 'This might have started out as a search, but it ended up as destruction for its own sake. Let's try the next room.'

What looked to have been a living room had been thoroughly trashed. It would have broken Smith's heart to see what had been done to his home. I sniffed at the air as I caught a trace of something, and then knelt down by the door to check the carpet.

'What is it?' said Penny.

'Blood,' I said. 'Just a small pool.'

'Oh, God. Lucy—'

'It wasn't our fault,' I said, getting to my feet again. 'We had no idea what we were sending her into.'

'Then why do you look so guilty?'

'Because I let Lucy being Black Heir cloud my judgement.

I just wanted to get rid of her for a while . . . I should have found something else for her to do.'

'She was so small . . .' said Penny.

'We don't know for sure that she's dead. There's not enough blood here to indicate a serious injury.'

'There could be more, somewhere else,' said Penny.

'Let's check the other rooms,' I said.

The bathroom, the kitchen and the study were even more of a mess. No more blood, but someone had really gone to town on the cottage, as though to make sure no one would ever want to live there again. Food and drink had been hurled around the kitchen and left dripping down the walls.

The study was the least disturbed of the rooms. Vincent Smith wrote his books there. His computer still stood on the simple wooden desk, apparently untouched, but his papers had been scattered across the floor. Penny knelt down and started sorting through them. Above the desk, two long shelves held a complete set of Smith's books. I checked the titles until I found the one about the UFO. A quick flick through revealed little in the way of evidence, and no conclusions.

I put the book back, picked up the overturned swivel chair and sat down before the computer. I fired it up, but all I could find on it were the manuscripts of his previous books. No encryptions, nothing password-protected, no personal stuff at all. I shut the computer down and looked at it thoughtfully.

As Ellie said, some men just live for their work.

'Anyone would think the man didn't have anything to hide,' I said.

'Most of these papers are research materials for Smith's latest book,' said Penny. 'Something about an old local legend of a hidden door that leads to a fairy kingdom.'

'I can't see anything in that to justify so much destruction,' I said.

Penny stood up and looked around the room.

'Somebody must have been convinced there was something here worth finding.'

'Then why didn't they take the computer with them?'

'What if they were only interested in Smith?' said Penny.

'They came here looking for him after he disappeared from the mortuary, and when they found he wasn't here, they took it out on Lucy.'

'The rooms may have been trashed,' I said. 'But there's no sign of any struggle. And Lucy would have known how to fight.'

'What about the blood?'

'There wasn't enough for a decent nose-bleed.'

Penny looked at me sharply. 'You think that means something?'

'It definitely means something,' I said.

'I'm worried about Lucy!' said Penny. 'Maybe we should tell the inspector she was here.'

'We can't report her missing,' I said. 'The inspector would want to know what Lucy was doing burgling a dead man's cottage, and how we knew she was here.'

'So we just abandon her?'

'We don't know for sure that anything has happened to Lucy,' I said steadily.

'You never liked her.'

'No,' I said. 'And that makes me feel even more guilty.'

Penny scowled. 'What do you think happened to Smith?'

'Some other group could have tracked him down before we did.'

'There can't be any other agents operating in the town,' said Penny. 'Ellie said we were the first new faces she'd seen in ages.'

'The whole point of secret groups,' I said patiently, 'is to go unnoticed.'

I sat back in my chair and stared at the blank screen of the computer, thinking hard, and then an idea hit me. I jumped up, went over to the window and looked out at the field.

'Did Smith buy this cottage because it was next to this particular field?' I said. 'Because he thought this might be where the starship crashed?'

Penny moved in beside me. 'Are you saying this field looks familiar?'

'No!' I said. 'It looks exactly like every other field! I'm just saying . . .'

I stopped and took a moment to get my emotions under control. Penny waited patiently, saying nothing.

'Sorry,' I said finally. 'I didn't mean to raise my voice. It's just . . . I am worried about Lucy. And I can't seem to get a grip on anything. Smith's life is like smoke.'

And then I stopped again.

'Wait a minute . . . I'm feeling something.'

'Ishmael, no one is watching us!'

'Not that. I'm feeling a presence. Vincent Smith . . . standing right where I'm standing, looking out of this window, at that field. Over and over again.'

'You can feel that?' said Penny.

'Yes,' I said.

'Are you sure it's not Smith's ghost?' said Penny.

'No,' I said. 'It's some kind of psychic impression. I'm only picking it up because the two of us are so similar.' I turned suddenly to grin at Penny. 'He really is the other crash survivor!'

'I'm not feeling anything,' Penny said carefully.

'Of course not,' I said. 'You're only human.'

Penny made calming gestures with both hands and chose her words carefully.

'Could this be like the wood? Something put in your head from outside?'

'You want more evidence?' I said. 'All right. There's something else in this room. I can feel it.'

I turned away from the window and looked quickly round the room. My eyes fell on a small pile of papers. I grabbed them and showed them to Penny.

'His last book, about the hidden door,' she said helpfully. 'You think that might be significant?'

'Not the book,' I said. 'Look at the papers!'

I showed her the golden stain soaked all down one edge.

'A paper cut,' I said. 'Smith had golden blood, just like me!'

I laughed out loud, relieved at having discovered some real evidence at last. Penny smiled with me, relieved that I was relieved.

'All right,' she said. 'What do we do now?'

I let the papers drop back on to the floor. 'We won't find anything else. I think we need to talk to Ellie again.'

'Oh dear,' said Penny. 'Really?'

'She knows everyone in town. She might be able to point us to someone else who knew Smith well.'

'And Lucy?'

'If she's out there, we'll find her,' I said. 'One way or another.'

NINE
Discovered in a Cemetery

I 'd thought Norton Hedley had run out of ways to surprise
me, until Penny and I stumbled across the little church in
the middle of town. A low stone wall surrounded a frankly
undersized graveyard, where row upon row of headstones
circled a squat stone building with stained-glass windows
but no steeple or spire. I leaned over the rusting iron gate to
study the tombstones. Some were so old they were little more
than moss-crusted shapes, their names and dates scoured
away by time and the elements. Other markers seemed more
recent but had been inscribed with so many names they all
but crowded each other off the limited space available. There
were no statues or monuments: just rank after rank of
perfectly standard stones, as though to suggest everyone was
equal in death.

'So many graves, so close together,' said Penny. 'There isn't
even any room for them to turn over.'

'This is what happens when one small cemetery has to
serve a very old town,' I said. 'Once they ran out of space,
I'll wager you good money they started planting them two
and three deep. With the topmost coffins, the lids are probably only a few inches under the soil. Step off the path, and
your foot would go right through.'

'Ishmael! The way your mind works!'

I smiled at her. 'I am now thinking about Jack-in-the-boxes
– and not in a good way.'

Penny smiled in spite of herself and turned her gaze back
to the overcrowded cemetery.

'You couldn't fit another body in there with a crowbar.'

I nodded. 'These days they probably only offer cremation
and scatter the ashes where you can.'

'That's sad,' said Penny.

'Not when the only alternative is to have your family members buried in another town,' I said. 'And Norton Hedley strikes me as a community that likes to keep itself very much to itself . . .'

'You're frowning again,' said Penny. 'What's wrong now?'

'None of the graves have any flowers on them,' I said. 'There's nothing here to indicate the local families pay any attention to their dead.'

Penny shrugged uncomfortably. 'Maybe they have other traditions.'

I tried the old gate, and its rusted-up hinges squealed protestingly as it moved under my hand.

'Ishmael?' said Penny. 'What are you doing?'

'I think we need to take a closer look.' I forced the gate all the way open, despite everything it could do to keep me out. Just another indication that this graveyard didn't get many visitors.

'What's the point?' Penny said bluntly, as she followed me in. 'It's not like there's anyone here we can question. Or, at least, not and expect any answers. In fact, if we do get a response, you'd better not stand between me and that gate.'

'I have a feeling . . .'

'Oh, please, not another feeling.'

'Pretty sure it's the same one,' I said. 'A nagging certainty that something important is going on in this town, that someone doesn't want me to know about.'

'Oh, well, as long as there's a sane and rational reason for intruding on people's last resting places,' said Penny.

'They won't notice,' I said. 'As long as we keep the noise down.'

I followed the single path as it meandered back and forth between the headstones, while Penny trudged rebelliously along in the rear. Gravel crunched under our feet, but no one emerged from the church to greet us or ask what we were doing.

'It's a peaceful enough setting, I suppose,' said Penny. 'Not a bad place to lay your bones down and get some rest.'

'You think so?' I said.

'Don't you?' said Penny.

'No,' I said. 'I don't think anything rests easily in Norton Hedley.'

Penny sighed. 'You see one ghost in a haunted house and suddenly you're an expert on the supernatural.'

'We are not alone here,' I said.

'Are you picking up psychic impressions again?'

'No,' I said. 'There's a woman tending a grave, over to your right.'

She'd been hidden from sight until now by a corner of the church. I stopped to look her over, while Penny moved in beside me. The woman must have known we were there, but she didn't acknowledge our presence.

'Let's get out of here,' Penny said quietly. 'We can always come back some other time.'

'She'll be gone by then,' I said, not lowering my voice. 'And I think she's the reason I was drawn to this place.'

Penny shook her head. 'Oh, this can only go well.'

She made a point of hanging back, as I led the way forward. I could feel her silent disapproval at intruding on someone's grief, but I was convinced this woman had something to tell me that I needed to know. The strength of the feeling disturbed me. I wasn't used to being driven by instincts. But ever since I'd come to Norton Hedley, the town seemed to be speaking to me on some level I didn't understand.

Or perhaps not the town, exactly . . .

We stopped just short of the grave, but the kneeling woman didn't so much as glance round, even when the sound of our feet on the gravel stopped right behind her. Small, drab and middle-aged, she was clearing faded flowers away so she could lay down some fresh ones. Huddled inside a battered old town coat, she was so thin there was hardly anything to her, and she wore a transparent plastic scarf stretched over her grey hair. I gave her a few moments to acknowledge us, but all her attention was fixed on sorting through the flowers. Penny put a hand on my arm.

'I really don't think we should bother her, Ishmael.'

'It's all right,' said the woman in a tired empty voice. 'I don't mind.'

She finished what she was doing and rose slowly to her

feet, wincing sharply as though her back troubled her. When she finally turned to face us, her gaze was calm and steady.

'I'm Ishmael Jones, and this is Penny Belcourt,' I said politely. 'We're just visiting the town.'

'I'm Muriel Lee. This is my daughter, Jackie.'

'I'm sorry,' I said. 'When did she die?'

'It's been nine years and four months,' said Muriel. 'I come here once a week to put some flowers down.'

'I don't see any flowers on the other graves,' I said.

'Ishmael!' said Penny.

'They don't do flowers here,' said Muriel. 'They don't even attend their own church that often. For a town steeped in weird stories, Norton Hedley has never been a religious community. Once they've buried their dead, they just move on. But I'm not local, so I can say to hell with the town and their ways.' She shook her head slowly. 'I wish to God I'd never come here.'

I got the feeling that while she was ready enough to talk, she didn't care who she was talking to. Anyone would do, to listen to a story she'd probably told many times before, for whatever small comfort it gave her. She gestured at the headstone with her handful of dead flowers.

'It's just a marker,' she said. 'There's no one in the grave because they never found my daughter's body.'

'We're very sorry to hear that,' said Penny. 'What happened to her?'

'She disappeared,' Muriel said flatly. 'After she'd become obsessed with finding the hidden door that opens on to the Other World.'

I glanced at Penny, both of us remembering the book Smith had been working on just before his death.

'That's part of the local folklore,' I said.

'Oh, yes,' said Muriel. 'One of the oldest stories they have. A long-lost door that can take you to a marvellous fairy world full of magic and wonders. But you have to be careful: spend a night there and you could return to find years have passed.'

'So people have returned?' I said.

'According to some of the stories,' said Muriel. 'Jackie read everything she could find about that door, and all the people who were supposed to have passed through it down the centuries.' She smiled sadly. 'She always said the Other World must be a truly wonderful place, because so few people ever wanted to come back. But then, Jackie never was very happy in this world.'

Muriel paused to stare reflectively at the gravestone. 'Her father had her declared legally dead and put this stone here. He had to pay off a lot of people to get permission; this cemetery is only supposed to be for people born in the town. But once it was done, and he'd appeased his conscience for not being here when it happened, he went away again. And never came back. Leaving me to put flowers on an empty grave every week because there's no one else to remember her.'

'Did your daughter ever say where she thought this door might be?' I said.

I didn't need to look at Penny to know she was glaring at me disapprovingly, but I could tell Muriel wanted to talk, and somehow I just knew I needed to hear what she had to say. As though something had guided my steps to this place and this moment. Muriel gave my question some thought before answering.

'She never told me, but then we never talked much. People here will tell you the door can be found anywhere, or that it will find you, if you want it badly enough. But according to the original stories, it's somewhere underneath the town. Deep down, in the dark, in the underworld.' She stopped to look at us carefully and see how we were reacting. 'Have you visited the wood outside the town?'

'Yes,' said Penny.

'I thought so,' said Muriel. 'I can see it in your eyes. You have reason to know how this place can change and turn on you. There are things here that don't belong in this world. Some say Norton Hedley was built over the door to hold it down and protect humanity from what it could do. Others insist the town was built to hide the door, so the people here could worship it in secret.' She smiled briefly. Just a quick grimace, with no humour in it. 'There are all kinds of stories in Norton Hedley.'

'Your daughter isn't the only one to go missing,' I said. 'People have been disappearing without a trace around here for centuries.'

'I knew that before I came here,' said Muriel. 'But I had no idea how many, and I never thought it could happen to my daughter.'

'Why does everyone stay, if so many people keep going missing?' said Penny. 'Why don't they just get out of here and go and live somewhere safe?'

'They stay because they were born here,' said Muriel. 'And they don't want to be anywhere else.'

'Do you believe this door actually exists?' I said.

'Oh, yes,' said Muriel.

'And the Other World?'

'Oh, yes,' said Muriel, quite casually. 'Though it's almost certainly not what most people think it is.'

'It does sound a bit much to take on trust,' I said.

'It's easier to believe in things like that when you're young,' said Muriel. 'Back when I was a lecturer in English folklore, I never believed in any of it. Until I came here to do research. I was so happy, at first. I thought I'd hit the motherload: enough new weird local folklore to base a career on. It never occurred to me to wonder why no one else had ever done this. But, of course, they had. I was just the latest in a long line of researchers to be seduced by Norton Hedley's siren song. And the town ate us all up and spat us out.'

She looked at her daughter's headstone for a long moment, her eyes lost and drowning in the past.

'Jackie never wanted to come here. She was seventeen then – such an awkward age. But her father was abroad on business again, and I promised her it would make a nice holiday before she went off to college in the autumn. She was all sulks at first, convinced she'd be bored out of her mind, away from all her friends. But I got her to help me with my research, and almost in spite of herself, she became interested. Out of all the local stories she could have picked, it had to be the door to the Other World. She read all the books I had, and then went off on her own in search of primary sources. I was so pleased that I'd finally awoken my daughter's interest in

my field. I encouraged her to dig deeper.' She smiled sadly at
the grave. 'So you could say that I did this to her.'

'What happened?' I said.

'Jackie went to the closest thing this town had to experts,'
said Muriel. 'The author Vincent Smith, and Frank Kendall at
the library. To be fair, Frank tried to warn her, but she wouldn't
listen. She thought she was hot on the trail, when really . . .
the door was dragging her in.

'Jackie would come home of an evening bubbling over with
some new detail or clue she'd dug up, and I was happy to
listen to her. Because I thought it was just another story. But
then she went out one evening and never came back. When I
tried to get people to do something, to help me find my missing
daughter, they just looked at me and said, "What did you
expect?"

'And now I'm trapped in this awful place. I have to stay,
because there's always the chance Jackie might turn up again
someday. I wonder how she'll look when she comes back
through the door. Whether she'll be the same age as when she
went away – and astonished to see how old I've become,
waiting for her.' She looked calmly at me and Penny. 'And
now you're here. Everyone is talking about you. Ellie's been
on the phone with her cronies ever since you showed up at
her hotel. All of them wondering what you're really up to.'

'We wanted to meet Vincent Smith,' I said. 'We're interested
in his books.'

'I knew Vincent,' said Muriel. 'I talked with him a lot. He
was very easy to talk to. I even helped him research his most
recent book, about the door.' She took in the expressions on
our faces and smiled briefly. 'I know; why would I want to
have anything to do with the legend that took my daughter
away from me? But I have to understand it if I'm to have any
hope of getting her back.'

I looked at her steadily. 'Did Smith tell you that might
happen?'

'No, he was always very careful never to raise any false
hopes. But he let me help him with his work because he could
see it helped me.' She broke off, as thoughts of the present
lured her back from the past. 'You must know that Vincent

died just the other day. But did you know his body has gone missing from the town mortuary? As though he simply got up and walked away.' The cold smile came and went. 'Vincent has become one of the weird stories of Norton Hedley. He'd have loved that. And as if that wasn't enough, the local undertaker, Winston Almond, dropped dead in the mortuary. For no obvious reason.'

Muriel shook her head slowly. 'Maybe he had to die, so Vincent could come back from the dead . . .' She realized from the look on our faces that she'd gone too far. 'I'm sorry. Spend too long in a cemetery and you're bound to end up with some odd ideas about death and life. And, of course, it's easy to believe in crazy things in a crazy town. Do yourselves a favour: get out of Norton Hedley while you still can. Before you end up trapped here, like me.'

She didn't wait for me or Penny to say anything, just thrust her dead flowers under one arm and walked unhurriedly out of the graveyard. She didn't look back once.

'Smith was researching a door to another world,' I said thoughtfully. 'And now he's vanished.'

'A door that's supposed to be deep underground,' said Penny. 'Maybe there's a reason why your ship chose to bury itself, apart from the obvious one.'

'Well done,' I said. 'You're becoming almost as paranoid as me.'

'It is starting to feel like something in this town is out to get us,' said Penny.

'Welcome to the world of creepy feelings,' I said. 'We have T-shirts and secret handshakes and everything.'

Penny fixed me with a stern look. 'Do you think this door really exists?'

'We've banged heads with stranger things.'

'But have you ever come face to face with a door that could take you to another world?'

I remembered the black hole on Brassknocker Hill and where it took me. I'd never told Penny, because there were things about that experience I still wasn't comfortable sharing with her.

'Not actual doors,' I said. 'But there are stories . . .'

'There are always stories,' Penny said impatiently. 'Do you believe in any of them?'

I shrugged. 'I don't *dis*believe.'

She shook her head. 'Would you just walk through a door, trusting there was a better place on the other side?'

'Not without a lot of convincing,' I said. 'And not without you.'

'Nice save,' said Penny.

And then we both looked round sharply as the rusty gate made loud protesting sounds, and a familiar figure entered the cemetery. He came striding through the tombstones to join us, paying no attention at all to the path, and Penny and I moved to stand even closer together.

Mr Whisper was a tall and imposing presence: broad-shouldered and barrel-chested, with a gleaming shaved head and skin so dark it had blue highlights. He wore a smart pinstripe suit, with white leather gloves and a yellow silk cravat. He looked very out of place in such a grave setting. But then, he always did.

He slammed to a halt and presented us with a convivial smile that didn't even come close to troubling his eyes. When he spoke, his voice was a harsh rasp, little more than a murmur.

'Mr Jones, Ms Belcourt! How delightful to meet the two of you again!'

I was so incensed I didn't even try to be polite.

'What are you doing here? I was promised complete freedom to operate on my own!'

Whisper smiled calmly back at me, entirely unmoved.

'I am aware of that, Mr Jones. I helped set all of this in motion, out of respect for your handling of the Harrow House affair. I trust the report the Colonel delivered was everything you hoped it would be? I thought it made for very interesting reading.'

'You read the file?' said Penny.

'Of course, dear lady.'

'Why are you interested in Norton Hedley?' I asked sharply.

'The town is not unknown to me, and to the Organization, Mr Jones.' Whisper flashed me his meaningless smile again.

'I should have known there was a reason I got so much cooperation,' I said bitterly. 'I didn't do you that big a favour.'

'Oh, believe me, I was extremely grateful,' said Whisper. 'But it is always helpful when one hand washes the other, professionally speaking.'

'Why are you here now?' Penny said bluntly.

'Although the Organization isn't interested in whatever it is you're doing here,' Whisper said easily, 'the same cannot be said for Black Heir. They have sent a field agent.'

'We know,' said Penny. 'Lucy Parker.'

'Then I trust you had enough sense to steer well clear of her,' said Whisper.

'Hold it,' I said. 'Lucy told us she'd been sent to provide assistance, with the Organization's knowledge.'

Whisper raised an elegant eyebrow. 'And you believed her?'

'She didn't have your permission to be here?' said Penny.

'Hardly, Ms Belcourt.'

'Then why did Black Heir send her?' I said. 'What's their game plan?'

Whisper produced an immaculate white handkerchief, dusted the top of a nearby tombstone and seated himself with magisterial aplomb.

'It would appear that Black Heir has concerns about your interest in this most unusual little town.'

'Why did you allow them to be a part of the investigation in the first place?' I said.

'Because they made such a fuss when they found out what we were doing,' said Whisper. 'It seems they regard the town as their own personal territory.'

'Because of the UFO that might have crashed here?' said Penny.

'Originally, no doubt,' said Whisper. 'We let them take part so we could keep an eye on them. And perhaps discover just what it is about this town that is so important to Black Heir.'

'I'm guessing that since you're here, any previous cooperation between the two groups has come to an end,' said Penny.

'Exactly, Ms Belcourt. Black Heir has stopped speaking to us and battened down their hatches, as though they have good reason to expect stormy weather.'

'The local hotel owner said some of the original team were really arrogant and unpleasant in their dealings with the townspeople,' I said. 'I assumed that was just standard Black Heir attitude, but now I have to wonder if they were trying to sabotage the investigation. When they discovered Penny and I were coming here anyway, they must have sent Lucy Parker to keep an eye on us.'

'And where is the young lady now?' said Whisper.

'She's disappeared,' said Penny. 'She could be dead.'

'I find it hard to believe she could be that obliging,' said Whisper.

'What is someone as high up in the Organization as you doing here, in person?' I asked bluntly.

'We want to know why such a small and isolated community has accumulated so many strange stories,' said Whisper. 'And why it holds the record for the most unexplained disappearances. Not just for this year, but every year since records began.'

'Why isn't this better known?' I said, frowning.

'Because Black Heir have gone to a great deal of trouble to suppress this information,' said Whisper.

'Why are they suddenly so interested in the weird stuff?' I said. 'It's not their usual territory. Are they planning to expand their sphere of influence? Or do they have reason to believe there's something special here?'

'The Organization would very much like to know the answers to those questions,' said Whisper. 'So we have decided to launch our own investigation.'

'If this is now an official mission,' I said carefully, 'does that mean I can call on your authority and protection?'

'Do you feel you need to?' said Whisper.

'Not yet. But—'

'Then we would prefer you remain uninvolved, for the time being,' said Whisper. 'Unless, of course, you are prepared to explain exactly why you are so interested in a minor author like Vincent Smith? No? I thought not. Well, we all have our secrets, do we not? Feel free to concentrate on your own business, Mr Jones, Ms Belcourt, and we will do the same.'

He got up from his tombstone, shot us one last unconvincing

smile and left the cemetery. Still not deigning to follow the winding gravel path. I looked at Penny.

'This case gets more complicated all the time.'

'His arrival will have set the whole town talking,' said Penny. 'If ever there was a man determined to stand out . . .'

'He does make an impression, doesn't he?' I said. 'I can't help thinking that's the point: to present an image to the world that most people can't help but remember, rather than see what's going on underneath.'

'So,' said Penny, 'Lucy wasn't on our side?'

'I never thought she was,' I said.

'I'm still worried about what might have happened to her,' said Penny. 'I mean, first Vincent Smith, then the undertaker, and now Lucy? Two might be a coincidence, but three times is enemy action.'

'And since Lucy is an experienced field agent, rather than the novice she pretended to be, she wouldn't have gone down without one hell of a fight,' I said. 'So if someone did ambush her, why couldn't we find any sign of a struggle in all that mess?'

'If someone or something has been disappearing people all these years, they must be really good at it by now,' said Penny.

'It would have to be something completely unexpected,' I said. 'Something even an experienced agent would never see coming.'

'We haven't seen anything,' said Penny.

'Perhaps it hasn't got close enough yet,' I said.

'Ishmael . . . what do you think is going on here?'

'I don't know,' I said slowly. 'But if it's important enough to attract the attention of both the Organization and Black Heir, I have to wonder who else might have chosen to get involved.'

Penny looked at me sharply. 'You think some other underground group might be operating here?'

'All it takes is for two groups to start squabbling over the same bone, and all the other big dogs will turn up to see if it's worth fighting over,' I said. 'And even though none of them are supposed to know it, my ship is buried here. Maybe I was called back to protect it.'

'But what happened to Smith and Almond and Lucy?' said Penny. 'And all the disappeared people?'

'I think this town happened to them.'

Penny nodded slowly. 'My head is full of burning wicker men.'

'Not to worry,' I said. 'It looks like rain.'

TEN

Answers to Questions

There are certain sounds you recognize even before you know what they are. They reach out to you, on a deep and primal level, and raise all the hackles on the back of your neck. Because some sounds are just hardwired into our survival instincts as something to be avoided.

Penny and I walked back to the hotel through streets so empty they made me feel like an intruder. The quiet was so complete it had a presence all its own, like a disapproving companion. But the feeling of being watched, of being observed by unfriendly unseen eyes, was no longer there. As though the town didn't care about us any more, because it had more important matters on its mind. So when the new sound appeared on the edges of my hearing, I slammed to a halt. Penny stopped with me, looked quickly around and then fixed me with a stern gaze.

'You've got that look on your face again. The one that says you've just noticed something that I haven't . . . and when I find out what it is, I'm really not going to like it.'

'That's a lot to read into one look,' I said.

'I'm used to it.'

'Listen,' I said.

'To what?' said Penny after a moment.

'There's a crowd around the next corner, between us and the hotel. And going by what I'm hearing, they are really not in the best of moods.'

'You and your alien senses.' Penny frowned, concentrating. 'I can't hear anything. Does it sound like a mob?'

'I don't think it's as straightforward as that.'

'Well, how big a crowd are we talking about?'

'Big enough to do some serious damage if they get angry enough.'

'What are they angry about? Can you hear what they're saying?'

'That's what's interesting. They're not saying anything. It's more like . . . the growl of a maddened animal.'

'OK . . .' said Penny. 'This town gets weirder by the moment.'

'It does, doesn't it?'

'Maybe we should seriously consider going somewhere else.'

'We have to get to the hotel.' I said. 'We need to talk to Ellie.'

'Is this another of your feelings?'

'Just common sense,' I said. 'People like Ellie always know everything that matters when it comes to small-town life.'

'But how are we supposed to get past a large angry crowd making animal noises?'

'I could always remove a thorn from their paw.'

Penny gave me a look, and I grinned.

'I think this could be our first clue as to what's wrong with this town. So far Norton Hedley has been very passive-aggressive, concealing its true nature by hiding its people from us. This is our first chance to confront the weirdness face to face.'

'What if it doesn't want to be confronted?' said Penny. 'The key words in angry mob are "angry" and "mob".'

'I'm sure they'll listen to reason.'

Penny shook her head. 'There are times when it amazes me that you've lasted this long. All right . . . Let's do this – before we have a rush of sanity to the head and think better of it. But if this goes wrong, I'm telling everyone it was your idea.'

'Try not to hold up the funeral too much.'

I started forward again, and Penny strode along beside me. As we drew nearer, the sound from the crowd grew louder and angrier: the massed voice of people on the edge and still pressing forward.

We rounded the corner and then stopped again. A huge crowd of townspeople had gathered outside the Pale Horse, filling up all the available space and spilling over into the side streets. So many people that my first thought was

So this is where everyone's got to. They stood shoulder to shoulder, packed close together, like the trees in the wood. Staring intently at the hotel, fixed in place like so many statues, with nothing in their body language to explain the terrible sound they were making.

I moved slowly closer, gesturing for Penny to stay behind me, and it was a sign of how disturbing the situation was that for once she didn't argue. The crowd was made up of men and women, young and old . . . all of them joined together in some unfathomable purpose. The sound issuing from hundreds of throats was a deep sustained growl, full of rage and menace, and it pulsed on the air like a living thing.

'That is a big crowd,' Penny said quietly.

'And definitely not in the mood to listen to outsiders,' I said.

'Why are they making that horrible sound?'

'Something has disturbed the town and stirred up its people. Driven them here, to confront whatever threatens them – and in so doing, to reveal something of the town's true nature.'

'Which is?'

'Beats the hell out of me.'

'They feel . . . more than normally angry,' said Penny.

'So now you're having feelings?'

'Not so much a feeling, more a raging certainty,' said Penny. 'This close, so much raw emotion is like being slapped in the face.'

'Something bad has happened inside the hotel,' I said.

Penny looked at me sharply. 'Could someone have come here, looking for us?'

'And then smashed the place up, like Smith's cottage, when they couldn't find us? Maybe.'

'Have we put people in danger by coming to this town?' asked Penny.

'No one was supposed to know we were here.'

'The Organization knew,' said Penny. 'And Black Heir. And spies will talk . . .'

'Perhaps we should ask the crowd what's going on,' I said.

Penny looked at the stiff and threatening backs of the crowd.

'I'm not sure anyone in there is at home to Mr Helpful. What if they turn on us?'

'I think they're too busy being angry about something else.'

'Maybe we should come back some other time,' said Penny. 'After the town has remembered where it left its sanity.'

'If something has happened in the Pale Horse that could cause an outbreak of weirdness like this, I want to know what it is,' I said.

'You don't think something could have happened to Ellie, do you?' Penny said suddenly. 'She was the only person in the hotel when we left.'

'If anyone came here looking for information, they wouldn't have needed to use force,' I said. 'Ellie would tell them everything they wanted to know, and a lot more besides.'

'Unless she didn't know what they wanted to know . . .'

I nodded slowly. 'I would feel better knowing she's all right. Come on, then; let's see if we can work our way through the crowd. Stick close to me and smile at everyone.'

'What if they don't smile back?'

'Smile harder.'

I advanced on the rear of the crowd, with Penny sticking very close to my side, and then we stopped abruptly as everyone in the back row suddenly turned around to stare at us. It was the same swift movement, carried out simultaneously by dozens of bodies moving in eerie synchronization. They stood very still, blocking our way, and while none of them said anything, they all had the same look in their eyes, and no expression at all on their faces. People with just a single thought on their minds and a single intent. I met the weight of the crowd's combined stare with my steadiest gaze; it felt as if it might be dangerous not to.

'What is this, Ishmael?' Penny said quietly. 'What is wrong with these people?'

'Remember that feeling I had, of being watched?' I said. 'This is how it felt.'

'You think the townspeople have been watching us all this time?'

'Not necessarily the people,' I said.

The massed growl from the crowd suddenly broke off, as

every man and woman turned as one to fix Penny and me with the same piercing gaze. The sense of massed rage and grievance had disappeared like a burst soap bubble, replaced by a fierce demand for information. And since I had no idea what they wanted to know, I just smiled determinedly back at them and started moving forward again. The townspeople fell back, their feet slamming down on the ground in perfect lockstep, as they opened up a narrow pathway for us to walk through. Penny thrust her arm through mine, pressing it hard against her side, and I squeezed it comfortingly. We walked on, into the midst of the beast.

Every head turned slowly to follow our progress, and I couldn't help but remember the old ordeal of running the gauntlet, where everyone waited for their chance to strike at the chosen victim. I pulled Penny in close, ready to protect her with my body if necessary, while my back crawled in anticipation of the blow I'd never see coming.

We finally reached the front of the crowd, and the door of the hotel loomed up before us. I wanted to just kick it in and charge through, but I didn't want to risk upsetting the mood of the crowd. They hadn't made a single sound since they became aware of Penny and me, but I could feel a pressure on the air, as though the crowd was expecting us to do something . . . and was ready to fall on us if we got it wrong. It was like being watched by a flock of birds in a Hitchcock movie. I turned slowly to face the crowd and raised my voice.

'What's happened here? Talk to us. Maybe we can help.'

The crowd just stared silently back, with the same cold and haunted look on every face. And then the door opened suddenly, to reveal Inspector Violet Silver standing calmly in the doorway. She studied Penny and me with her usual sleepy gaze, as though possessed and potentially dangerous crowds appeared every day. She nodded easily at the watching faces.

'Don't let them throw you; they're just interested. You'd better come inside.'

She stepped back to let us pass, and I gestured for Penny to go first while I kept an eye on the crowd. She hurried in and I followed after her, almost treading on her heels. Violet stared thoughtfully out at the crowd, as though she wanted to order them to disperse and go home. But she didn't, because she knew they wouldn't. She studied the crowd with an expression almost as unreadable as theirs, and then closed the door in their faces.

With the pressure of the crowd's gaze removed, it felt as if a great weight had been lifted off me. The lobby was empty, and there was a fragile calm on the air – like the stillness that precedes a storm. I remembered Mr Whisper informing us that Black Heir were preparing for stormy weather. Penny tugged at my arm.

'Ishmael, Ellie isn't behind the reception desk.'

'She's probably in the bar,' I said.

'Not this time, Mr Jones,' said Violet. She sounded so tired that even talking was an effort. 'It's a good thing the two of you turned up. Saved me the trouble of having to come and find you.'

'What is going on here?' said Penny. 'Why are all those people gathered outside, and what the hell is wrong with them?'

'Don't you know?' said Violet.

'Obviously not,' I said.

'Then why did you come back here?'

I looked at her for a moment. It hadn't sounded like a casual question.

'Because we have some more questions for Ellie, about Vincent Smith. She said they were friends.'

Violet smiled briefly. 'Ellie was everybody's friend, as long as there was money in it.'

'Were the two of them close?' said Penny.

'They're close enough now,' said Violet. 'They're both dead.'

Penny and I looked at each other sharply. Violet caught that, with eyes that only seemed sleepy.

'How did Ellie die?' I said.

'I came back here looking for you,' said Violet. 'And found Ellie lying slumped over the desk. I checked for life signs, but it was obvious she was dead. And not a mark on her anywhere . . . just like Vincent Smith and Winston Almond.' She shook her head slowly. 'Three heart attacks, so close together? I don't think so . . . I've moved the body out back, so I can examine her.'

'You moved the body?' I said. 'You're stronger than you look.'

'I do a lot of weeding,' said Violet.

'But why would you compromise a crime scene?'

'That's a very professional question for an amateur UFO spotter,' said Violet.

'He used to love all those CSI shows,' said Penny.

'It's true,' I said. 'I really did. Especially the weird ones.'

Behind her heavy-lidded gaze, Violet was studying me carefully.

'The crime scene people finally got in touch to tell me they won't be here for at least three days. So if there was evidence on the body, I was going to have to find it myself.'

I nodded understandingly. 'And would I be right in saying that you haven't found anything to suggest how Ellie died?'

'Not a thing,' said Violet. 'It's as though she just dropped down dead where she was, for no reason.'

'But that's not what you believe,' I said.

'It's my job to be suspicious,' said Violet, almost apologetically.

'So what did happen to Ellie?' said Penny.

'Presumably, the same thing that happened to Mr Smith and Mr Almond,' said Violet. She looked thoughtfully at Penny and me. 'Do you have any idea how they might have died?'

'I think something very bad and very dangerous has come to your little town, Inspector,' I said.

She surprised me then with a cold and caustic smile. 'Norton Hedley can look after itself.'

'What is it that makes this town so different, Inspector?' I said.

'Years of going its own way,' said Violet. 'In particular, no one has killed another person in Norton Hedley since 1928. And that was an outsider.'

'But you do have a hell of a lot of unexplained disappear-ances,' I said.

'You've been doing your homework,' Violet said admiringly. 'And yet . . . you don't seem too surprised, or even upset, that Ellie is dead.'

'I'm not one for showing my feelings,' I said.

'That's true; he isn't,' said Penny. 'But we are both very sorry to hear that Ellie has been murdered.'

Violet raised an eyebrow. 'I don't believe I used that word. Do you know something I don't, Ms Belcourt?'

Penny smiled at her sweetly. 'You'd be amazed what I know, Inspector.'

'You know something about what's going on,' said Violet.

'We didn't plan for any of this,' said Penny.

Violet turned her heavy gaze on me. 'What have the two of you been doing since you left here?'

'Just checking out the town, and walking up and down in it,' I said.

'Of course,' said Violet. 'You are tourists, after all. Where did you go, exactly?'

'All over the place,' said Penny. 'We went to see Frank Kendall at the library, and then took a stroll through the wood . . .'

'People have been known to see things in the wood,' Violet said casually.

'Really?' Penny said innocently. 'What kind of things?'

Violet just smiled her tired smile. 'And where did you go next?'

'Vincent Smith's cottage,' said Penny.

'But you already knew he was dead,' said Violet.

'We wanted to see something, after coming all this way,' said Penny.

'Oh, of course,' said Violet. 'I hope you got some nice photos.'

'It was very picturesque,' said Penny.

Listening to them spar was like watching tennis. I felt like applauding both sides.

'After that,' said Penny, 'we took a look round the cemetery.'

'All the local beauty spots,' Violet said approvingly. 'You've covered a lot of ground for one day, going back and forth. Were you searching for anything in particular?'

'Just looking,' I said.

'Don't you find it just a bit odd that all the bad stuff starts happening the day you arrive in town?' said Violet.

I raised an eyebrow. 'This town has a long history of odd things happening. That's one of the reasons we came here.'

'But three people have died in suspicious circumstances since you arrived,' said Violet, not at all accusingly.

'Three people?' said Penny. 'Are you telling us Vincent Smith didn't die of a heart attack, after all?'

'How very sharp of you, Ms Belcourt,' said Violet. 'But it's hard to be sure of anything when there isn't any evidence.'

'Where did you put Ellie?' I asked.

Violet gestured at the reception desk. 'There's a private room, out back.'

'I need to take a look at the body,' I said.

Violet smiled slowly, as though she'd trapped me into admitting something.

'And why should I allow that, Mr Jones?'

'Because you don't have anyone to get you your evidence,' I said. 'And because you're curious to see what I'll do.'

I headed for the reception desk, and Penny immediately moved in close behind me, to keep Violet at a distance. A door behind the desk gave on to a pokey little parlour, with ugly furniture and cheap prints on the walls. Ellie's body had been neatly laid out on the sofa. She looked smaller and more fragile, without her overbearing personality to hold the attention. Like a broken doll, that someone couldn't be bothered to throw away. I checked for a pulse in her neck, knowing I wouldn't find one.

'You're not bothered by dead bodies, then, Mr Jones?' Violet said casually. 'Only most people are.'

'This isn't my first murder,' I said.

'What exciting times you must have, as a tourist,' said Violet.

'I'm not a tourist,' I said, not looking round. 'You know that, Inspector.'

'I do now,' said Violet.

I examined the body carefully, speaking my thoughts out loud for Violet's benefit.

'The body is warm and presents no signs of rigor mortis. Hardly surprising, given that Penny and I talked to Ellie not that long ago. Her face shows no sign of shock or pain. In fact, her makeup is immaculate, and her hair undisturbed. There are no signs of violence on the body, and no obvious injuries to suggest she tried to defend herself.'

'You've done this before,' Violet said admiringly.

'More times than I care to remember,' I said. I pulled Ellie's mouth open, leaned over and had a good sniff. 'I'm not picking up any traces of poison.'

'You can do that?' said Violet.

'Oh, he can,' said Penny. 'Don't worry about being freaked out; I never get used to it.'

'So you've been involved with murders as well, Ms Belcourt?' said Violet.

'Many times,' said Penny. 'Since we've apparently started being honest with each other, even though nobody asked me whether I thought that was a good idea.'

'Hush,' I said. 'Working.' I straightened up again and looked thoughtfully at the body. 'How old was Ellie?'

'Forty-seven,' said Violet. 'The same age as me.'

'Of course,' I said. 'You were at school together. I think we can agree her age wasn't a factor in this. Were you close?'

'Couldn't stand the woman,' said Violet.

I turned to look at her, careful not to smile. 'Did you kill Ellie, Inspector?'

'No,' she said steadily.

'I had to ask. You know how it is.' I turned back to the body. 'Let's review the nature of the three deaths. First, Vincent Smith died of an apparent heart attack, which, without medical confirmation, is just another way of saying he was found dead from no obvious cause. Then Winston Almond turns up dead in the mortuary under the same conditions. And now Ellie makes three.'

'Don't forget Lucy,' said Penny.

'Trust me, I haven't forgotten her,' I said. 'But she's just missing, until we find a body.'

'Lucy?' said Violet. 'I don't think I know that name.'

'A colleague, of sorts,' I said. 'We met briefly in the town, earlier on, but now she seems to have vanished. Like a great many other people around here.'

'So that makes a fourth possible death, linked to you,' said Violet.

'Oh, I'm sure she'll turn up,' I said. 'Bad pennies always do.' I thought for a moment. 'When you discovered Ellie's body, were there any signs of a struggle in the lobby?'

'No,' said Violet. 'Nothing to show anyone had been there. But it's always possible Ellie knew her killer and didn't see them as a threat. Until it was too late.'

I didn't need to turn round to know Violet was looking meaningfully at me and Penny.

'Anyone in the town could fit that description,' I said. 'And she'd have more reason to trust them than us. I searched the mortuary earlier and didn't find anything suspicious there either. In my experience, people who know how to come and go from a crime scene without leaving any clues are usually professionals.'

'In your experience?' Violet said diffidently. 'And what experience would that be, Mr Jones?'

'I've been around,' I said. 'Now, Vincent Smith, Winston Almond and Ellie Markham – what did all three of them have in common?'

'They're all local,' Violet said thoughtfully. 'Though, strictly speaking, you're not accepted as local here unless you were actually born in the town, like Ellie. I came here as a child, and I'm still not considered local. Vincent arrived in the sixties as a young man, and Winston moved in to take over the local undertaking business some five years ago.'

'Different ages, different backgrounds,' I said. 'Did Vincent know Winston?'

'Oh, yes,' said Violet. 'Winston never missed one of Vincent's evening sessions in the bar.'

'Then that's what the three of them have in common,' I said. 'Vincent Smith.'

I stood there for a while, thinking, while Penny and Violet looked at me expectantly.

'Well?' Violet said finally.

'Well what?' I said.

'Have you come to any conclusions?'

'Not yet.'

'Do you think you're going to?'

'Who can say?'

'I think anyone would agree that I have been extraordinarily patient with you,' Violet said heavily.

'Patient and beyond,' I said.

'But enough is more than enough. It's time for you to answer some questions, Mr Jones.'

I smiled at her. 'Of course, Inspector. But I can't guarantee that you'll like the answers.'

Violet fixed me with a thoughtful stare and, just like that, she didn't look sleepy any more.

'According to the police computers, your driving licence is a fake.'

'That was quick,' I said.

'You get preferential treatment when it's a murder. I notice you're not denying it.'

'What would be the point?' I said.

'In fact, there's no trace of you anywhere in the system, Mr Ishmael Jones. No birth certificate, no employment history, no tax records. Officially, you don't exist.'

'And yet I'm standing right here in front of you.'

Violet just nodded. I had to admire her self-control. I've had authority figures tearing their hair out and throwing heavy objects at me under far less provocation. Violet considered the situation, glanced at Penny and then fixed me with a challenging stare.

'I need to talk to you in private.'

'Am I under arrest?' I said politely.

'Only if you don't cooperate.'

'Am I a suspect?'

'You always were,' said Violet. 'Agree to talk, and we can have our little chat right here.'

'You don't want to drag me off in handcuffs?' I said. 'How refreshing.'

'Norton Hedley is too small to have its own police station,' said Violet.

'And yet it has its own mortuary,' said Penny.

Violet and I both looked at her, and she shrugged quickly. 'Just saying . . .'

'You can wait outside, Ms Belcourt,' said Violet. 'But don't go anywhere. I'll have some questions for you, once I'm done with him.'

'You can talk to me right now,' said Penny. 'Because I'm not leaving Ishmael alone with you.'

'I am a detective inspector,' said Violet.

'Guess how much I don't care.'

'There's no need for any unpleasantness,' I said quickly. 'Penny, I think the inspector might find it easier to cope with some of the things I have to say if we do this in private. You know what I'm talking about . . .'

'I don't,' said Violet.

'You will,' I said. I looked directly at Penny. 'You can stay right outside the door, and I promise I'll call you in if there's any police brutality.'

Penny scowled. 'You had better tell me everything, afterwards.'

'Of course,' I said.

'Everything!'

'I promise.'

Penny turned her scowl on Violet. 'Get this straight: he belongs to me. You mess with him and I will punch a hole in the wall with you.'

She stormed out of the room, slamming the door behind her.

'I think she means it,' said Violet.

'She's very protective.'

'I wouldn't have thought you needed protecting.'

'I keep telling her that,' I said.

'I always knew there was something different about you, Mr Jones.'

'You're very observant.'

'All part of the training, to pay attention to details,' said Violet. She put her back against the door, casually blocking the only exit. She seemed entirely calm and at ease, but I could sense wheels turning in her head as she worked her way slowly and logically to an inevitable conclusion. 'You're always watching the world, as though you don't trust it. As though you've had bad experiences in your past, and good reason to expect more in the present. You watch people as though you don't always understand them – or, at least, not what moves and motivates them. Like you're an outsider, and always will be. Where are you from, Mr Jones?'

'Not from around here,' I said.

'And then there's Ms Belcourt . . . The way she looks at you. As if she trusts you implicitly and is always ready to back you up . . . But also half expecting you to say something wrong or give something away.' She considered me for a long moment, as though deciding whether to commit herself . . . And then I saw her back away from where her thoughts were taking her, because it was just too big a leap for her to take.

'You didn't just happen to come here,' she said slowly. 'I've met real UFO enthusiasts – you can't avoid them in this town – and you two just aren't weird enough. I know a cover story when I hear one.'

'I came here to talk to Vincent Smith,' I said.

'But he was never anyone special,' said Violet. 'What could he possibly have known that you needed to know so badly?'

'That's what I was going to ask him,' I said.

'Who are you, really?' said Violet.

'I'm nobody,' I said. 'Ask your computers.'

'Everyone's somebody. The only people who can keep their identity completely secret these days are security, military or terrorist,' said Violet. 'So which are you?'

'None of the above,' I said. 'I'm just someone who's taken a special interest in your odd little town. For a while, I thought I was here to solve the mystery of Vincent Smith's death, but now I think I'm here to solve the mystery of Norton Hedley. Do you have any idea just how strange your town is, Inspector?'

'Every town has its weird side,' said Violet.

'But Norton Hedley is industrial-strength strange,' I said. 'And then there's all the townspeople who've disappeared, without trace or explanation. How can you simply accept so many people going missing, Inspector?'

'The last time I raised the matter with my superiors, I was

ordered to drop it,' said Violet. 'It was also made very clear to me that if I tried to pursue the matter, it would mean the end of my career.'

'And why do you think that was?'

'Because someone dropped the hard word on my superiors,' Violet said flatly. 'Someone much higher up the food chain doesn't want it investigated.'

'Give me room to work, and I'll get you some answers,' I said. 'I might even be able to do something about the problem itself.'

Violet couldn't help but raise an eyebrow, even as she clung to her practised composure.

'You really think you can solve a mystery that goes back centuries?'

I smiled. 'Mysteries are my stock in trade.'

'I asked the wrong question, didn't I?' said Violet. 'Not *who* are you, but *what* are you?'

I just smiled, acknowledging the point.

She sighed heavily, as though struggling with an entirely unfair burden.

'I'm supposed to be getting information out of you.'

'Go ahead,' I said. 'Ask me something.'

'And you'll answer?'

'If I can.'

'Did you kill these three people?'

'No,' I said.

'Do you know who did?'

'I have suspicions, but no evidence.'

'Who are you working for?' Violet said finally, with an air of being ready to settle for anything.

'This was supposed to be an entirely private matter. I didn't expect any of this.'

'You were the one who broke into the mortuary,' said Violet, with the air of someone reluctantly surrendering an ace. 'You were seen leaving, just before Almond's body was discovered.'

'Seen by whom?' I said.

'It was an anonymous tip,' said Violet.

'Of course it was,' I said. 'I went to the mortuary to check whether Smith really was dead, but his body was gone by the time Penny and I got there. And the undertaker was already deceased.'

'You expect me to just take your word for that?' said Violet, sounding genuinely exhausted after all the hoops I'd made her jump through.

'Why would I lie?'

'You tell me.'

'You're assuming the same person is responsible for all three deaths,' I said. 'But Vincent died the day before I got here.'

'The day you say you got here,' said Violet. 'You could have sneaked into town yesterday, and then made a big deal out of arriving at the railway station today.'

I decided it was my turn to raise an eyebrow. 'Does that even sound likely?'

'I've lost track of what's likely in this case,' Violet said sadly.

'Keep digging,' I said encouragingly.

'I read the book Vincent wrote about the UFO,' said Violet. 'He spent years searching for evidence of a crash site, but he never found anything. What made you think you could do any better?'

'Perhaps I'm more motivated.'

'Why are you so interested in Vincent?' said Violet. 'He could tell a good story, but even he would have admitted he was no authority.'

'I might have met him here once, in the past,' I said.

Violet looked at me sharply, so taken with finally establishing a connection that she forgot all about appearing sleepy.

'You've been to Norton Hedley before?'

'It was a long time ago.'

'What were you doing here?'

'Just passing through.'

Violet shook her head. 'You're never going to give me a straight answer, are you?'

'Not if I can help it,' I said cheerfully.

'Why?' said Violet, just a bit desperately.

I met her gaze steadily. 'Because what you don't know can't come back to bite you.'

'I knew it,' said Violet. 'You're security.'

'Let's just say that I could pass for one, in the dark.'

'Bearing in mind that you are the only real suspect I've got,' said Violet, 'give me one good reason why I shouldn't just arrest you?'

'Because you don't have anywhere to lock me up.'

'I could find somewhere.'

I smiled at her. 'I'd be gone by the time you got back.'

'I have a crowd of very upset townspeople outside, who would be only too happy to help me subdue you,' said Violet. 'If I said you were giving me trouble.'

'I don't think they're in a mood to listen to anyone,' I said. 'Apart from whoever it is that's pulling their strings. Do you have any idea who that might be?'

'No,' said Violet.

'Have you ever seen this phenomenon before?'

'I've heard stories.'

'This town is lousy with stories,' I said. 'Which one are we talking about?'

'That the town will come together to defend itself if it feels under threat.'

'Now that is interesting,' I said. 'You said *town* – not townspeople.'

'Same thing,' said Violet.

'Not necessarily.'

'Do you know what's going on here?' Violet said bluntly.

'Not yet,' I said. 'But I'm working on it.'

Violet met my gaze steadily. 'Who are you, really?'

I felt I owed her something, so I gave her as much of the truth as I thought she could handle.

'I work for a group you've never heard of. We specialize in investigating the weird and uncanny, and then doing something about them.'

'All right,' said Violet. 'I'll give you enough rope to hang yourself . . . or somebody else. But don't even think about leaving town.'

'Wouldn't dream of it,' I said. 'Not until I've uncovered the truth about Norton Hedley.'

'Better men than you have tried,' said Violet.

I had to smile. 'You've never met anyone like me.'

*   *   *

When I opened the parlour door, Penny was standing right outside. I nearly walked into her.

'You've been eavesdropping,' I said.

'Of course,' said Penny.

'Well done,' I said.

Penny glared past me, at Violet. 'Did she give you any trouble?'

'We have decided to be civilized,' I said, 'and not get in each other's way.'

'That's your version,' said Violet. 'My version is that I'm letting you go because I don't have enough evidence yet to arrest you. Now I'd better go and talk to the crowd, and tell them not to bother you.'

'I think that would be safest,' I said. 'For all concerned.'

'What is wrong with those people?' said Penny.

'It's the town,' said Violet.

She led the way back through the lobby and out of the hotel. The crowd was right where we'd left them, still facing the front door. They didn't appear to have moved a muscle. Now I knew what to look for, I could see the occupying presence in their faces: someone else watching me, through the townspeople's eyes. I had to fight down an urge to wave cheerfully back. Perhaps Violet saw something of that in my face, because she quickly stepped forward to address the crowd.

'It's not them.'

The crowd looked unconvinced, but didn't argue. I was intrigued that they seemed willing to accept her word, if not her authority. The townspeople fell back as one, opening up a new path. I moved steadily forward, with Penny sticking so close she was practically climbing inside my pocket, and we passed quickly through the crowd and off down the street. I didn't look back, because I could still feel the pressure of the crowd's gaze on my back, like the red dot from a sniper's rifle.

The moment we rounded the far corner, I broke into a run, and Penny was right there with me. I kept up a good pace and didn't stop until we were several empty streets away. I put my back against a wall so I could see in all directions at once, and waited patiently while Penny bent over and struggled to

get her breathing back under control. Sweat ran down her face
and dripped on to the pavement.

'I really don't like being the subject of public attention,' I
said after a while. 'Especially by people who might not be
entirely in their own minds.'

Penny straightened up, breathing steadily, and mopped at
her face with a handkerchief.

'Why is it you never get out of breath? That is seriously
spooky.'

'Better living through alien technology,' I said calmly. 'Take
your time; no one's coming after us. I'd hear them.'

'What happened between you and Inspector Silver?' said
Penny.

'I thought you were listening?'

'I tried,' said Penny. 'I had my ear pressed right up against
the door, but I couldn't hear a damned thing. I was ready to
rush in there and rescue you if it had gone on much longer.'

'Nice to know,' I said.

I took her through the gist of what was said, and she
nodded thoughtfully.

'How much time do you think we have before she runs
out of patience and yells for reinforcements?'

'Not a lot,' I said. 'She's only letting us run free now
because she doesn't know what else to do.'

'Please tell me you have a scheme in mind – preferably one
that doesn't involve any more running.'

'It's hard to make plans when you don't have any hard
information to work with,' I said. 'There were no clues left
on Ellie's body, just like the undertaker in the mortuary.
Nothing to point me in any direction . . . Our killer is being
very careful. And I mean careful on a professional level.'

'I've been thinking,' said Penny. 'Because when you're
stuck on the wrong side of a door, there's not much else you
can do to keep busy. What if all of this is nothing to do with
you or the crashed ship? What if the deaths are just the work
of some local murderer, killing for his own reasons?'

'We can't assume that,' I said.

'Why not?'

'Because then we'd be left with nothing to work on,' I said.

'Anyway, it would be one hell of a coincidence, if some local headcase decided to start his murder spree just as we wandered into town.'

'Coincidences do happen,' said Penny.

'Not in this town,' I said. 'Besides, I've got a feeling about this.'

Penny smiled. 'Of course you have, space boy.'

'Then let's concentrate on the mystery, spy girl.'

'All right, then . . . Could all of these people have died because someone came to this town looking for information about Vincent Smith and killed them when they couldn't or wouldn't cooperate?'

I looked at her sharply. 'If someone has been taking note of who we've been talking to, we'd better get back to Frank. Before someone else does.'

When we finally arrived at the library, the door was locked. I hit it with my shoulder and the door all but jumped off its hinges. I stepped inside and sniffed at the air.

'Someone has died here,' I said quietly.

'Is it Frank?' said Penny, just as quietly.

I concentrated on the scent. 'Yes.'

'Damn. I liked him.'

'And . . . There's someone else with him.'

I led the way quickly through the maze of bookshelves, and when we emerged by the main desk, Frank was lying dead on the floor. An elderly man was kneeling beside him, gently patting Frank's shoulder, as though to comfort him for being dead.

'Hello, Ishmael,' said Vincent Smith. 'I've been expecting you.'

He got up slowly, like the old man he seemed to be, and looked me over carefully. He didn't even glance at Penny.

She glared at him. 'Did you kill Frank?'

'Of course not,' said Vincent, still giving me his full attention. 'He was my friend.'

'If you were expecting Ishmael,' Penny said forcefully, 'why didn't you make yourself known to him?'

He finally turned to look at her, as though she was some urchin who'd tugged at the king's cloak.

'Because I didn't know why he was here,' he said calmly. 'I couldn't be sure what being human for so long might have done to his mind.'

'You say that like it's a bad thing,' said Penny.

'It can be,' said Vincent. He smiled briefly. 'Look what it did to me.'

'So,' I said. 'You're not dead, after all.'

He just nodded, not offering any apology. I'd come a long way to meet him, with so many questions . . . but now that we were finally standing face to face, I didn't know what to say. He looked completely ordinary: just a stooped old man with a deeply lined face and thinning white hair, dressed in a faded grey suit. But he still had a strength and a presence, for all his years. Like a man who knew things, but guarded his secrets because no one else was worthy of them.

He gestured at the three chairs Frank had set out earlier. He barely waited for me to nod, before walking over to them. I went after him. Penny scowled at me for letting Vincent take the lead. I knew he was deliberately keeping us off balance, so he could control the situation, but I was ready to go along, for the moment. It might prove easier to get some answers out of him that way. We all chose a chair and sat down. Vincent took some time, arranging his old bones comfortably, before he finally smiled at me.

'I always knew you'd find me, some day.'

'It wasn't easy,' I said. 'I didn't even know you existed until very recently.'

'I know,' said Vincent. 'I felt it when the barrier between us suddenly disappeared.'

'Did you put it there?' I said.

'No. That was the transformation machines. I was lucky to get to them first, while most of their systems were still working. By the time they got to you, they were falling apart. But given the shape the ship was in after the crash, we're both lucky to be alive.'

'Why didn't you stick with me when we left the ship?' I said. 'Why did you never try to find me?'

'When you're hiding out in an alien world, you survive by keeping your head down.'

'Why did you pretend to be dead when I came looking for you?'

'Because he was hiding from the killer,' said Penny.

For the first time, Vincent looked at her directly. 'Exactly.'

'This is my partner, Penny,' I said.

Vincent looked at both of us and smiled briefly at me. 'You've gone native.'

'And you haven't?' I said.

'I've enjoyed my time here,' said Vincent. 'But I never forgot who I am.'

I could have said many things in response to that, but I made myself concentrate on what was important.

'Do you know where our ship is?'

'Of course,' said Vincent. 'I watched it bury itself. I spent a long time waiting for the self-repair mechanisms to finish their work, until it became clear that the damage was so severe the ship wouldn't be going anywhere. Fortunately, by that time my research into the town's unusual history had led me to another way out: the door to Other Worlds.'

I leaned forward in my chair. 'Are you saying you've found it? And it really can transport people to other places?'

'It's the door to anywhere,' said Vincent. 'And it's our way home.'

'Do you know exactly where the door is?' said Penny.

Vincent seemed a little irritated at having his word questioned.

'It's deep under the wood. Not far from where the ship crashed.'

'Then why haven't you used it before now?' said Penny.

'Because I'd grown fond of this town and its people.' Vincent smiled at me. 'You know how it is. You grow attached to things.'

'So you went native as well,' I said.

He nodded slowly. 'I suppose I did.'

'What made you go looking for the door?' said Penny.

'I already knew it was here,' said Vincent.

'Is the door why we came to Earth in the first place?' I said.

Vincent glanced at Penny. 'Not in front of the natives.'

'She's my partner,' I said flatly.

'Not all our secrets are ours to share,' said Vincent. 'And right now, we need to concentrate on the killer who has come here in pursuit of me and you.'

'Do you know who it is?' I said.

'I've hidden from any number of secret groups down the years,' said Vincent. 'Black Heir has always been the most persistent. And now they've sent one of their field agents.'

'We know about Lucy Parker,' said Penny. 'We thought she'd been sent to assist us, but—'

'I never trusted her,' I said.

'You did too!' said Penny.

'Not really,' I said. 'She said that her assignment was only agreed on at the last moment, while you and I were travelling here on the train. But she also said she'd arrived in town the day before. So if she wasn't telling the truth about that, how could I trust anything she said?'

'You always were a great one for paying attention,' said Penny. 'But if you knew she wasn't trustworthy, why didn't you say anything?'

'We had other things on our minds,' I said.

'We're partners,' said Penny. 'That means you share.'

'Do you always let her talk to you like that?' said Vincent.

'We're partners,' I said. 'It comes with the territory.'

'I wouldn't know,' said Vincent. 'Where is this Black Heir agent?'

'We don't know,' said Penny. 'She's gone missing.'

'I sent her to search your cottage, to give her something to do,' I said. 'Sorry about that.'

'Not to worry,' said Vincent. 'I never kept anything important there. You'd be surprised what cleaning ladies notice.'

'But when we went to your place, there was no sign of Lucy anywhere,' I said.

'Perhaps she thought you'd sent her off on a wild goose chase,' said Vincent. 'She could be hiding out somewhere while she waits for new instructions from her controller on who to kill next.'

Penny shook her head immediately. 'Lucy didn't strike me as a killer.'

Vincent ignored her, concentrating on me. 'She's Black Heir. You know what that means. How many crash survivors have they killed to get their hands on new alien tech?'

Penny stared at me. 'Did you know about this, back when you worked for Black Heir?'

I met her gaze steadily. 'There were rumours, but I never saw anything.'

'You worked for those vultures?' said Vincent.

'I was left alone in the world,' I said. 'I needed powerful groups to protect me. And I was able to do good work, for Black Heir and others.'

Vincent shook his head. 'I have had enough of this world. I'm not waiting for the killer to find me; I'm going home. Come with me, Ishmael. You don't belong in this world any more than I do.'

'You're going to use the door?' I said.

'It can send us where we belong,' said Vincent. And then he nodded at Penny. 'You do realize you can't take your pet with you?'

Penny turned to me, waiting for me to defend her, and then looked shocked when I just smiled comfortingly at her, before giving Vincent my full attention.

'I'm not going anywhere,' I said, 'until you tell me the truth about what we're doing here.'

'Then ask,' said Vincent.

'We were both made human at the same time, so why do you look your age, and I don't?'

Vincent's face seemed to melt and run, until suddenly it snapped into a new focus . . . and just like that, he looked the same age as me. He stretched slowly, laughing softly.

'I have complete control over this body, courtesy of the transformation machines. Getting older on the outside, while staying young within. Appearing to age at the proper rate allowed me to stay in this little community and not stand out.'

'What if you'd had to stay longer than you could have aged normally?' said Penny.

'Then I would die and come back as my own son or grandson.'

'Leaving your friends to grieve?' said Penny.

'There's nothing like living a long life to teach you to look forward, not back,' said Vincent.

'What made you decide it was time to fake your death?' I said.

'A great many people had appeared in the town, asking questions,' said Vincent. 'I watched, from a safe distance, and recognized some of them as Black Heir field agents.'

'Hold it,' said Penny. 'How were you able to recognize agents from one particular underground group?'

Vincent shot me an impatient *Do I really have to answer all these questions?* look, and I gave him a look in return that said, *Yes, you do.*

'After the ship crashed, I left this town and went out into the world,' said Vincent.

'Why didn't we leave together?' I said.

'I had to make sure the damaged ship was able to conceal itself successfully,' said Vincent. 'By then, you'd disappeared. So I left town on my own. The machines had briefed me on all the underground groups, so I spent some time watching them carefully, from a distance. When I was convinced they didn't know about me, I returned to Norton Hedley as Vincent Smith. And I've stayed here ever since.'

'Because it was safe?' I said.

'Because of the door.'

'What is so important about this door?' I said.

Vincent glanced at Penny. 'Not now, Ishmael.'

'Why not now?' said Penny. 'Why can't I know?'

'Because you're only human,' said Vincent.

Penny rounded on me, her face flushed with anger. 'Ishmael, say something!'

'Hush,' I said. 'This is important.'

Vincent carried on as though nothing had happened, and perhaps for him, nothing had.

'I was worried these new agents might come looking for me, so I decided the best way to avoid suspicion was to be dead. Complete control over my body includes all kinds of useful tricks. I didn't think Black Heir would bother me if I was lying stiff and cold on a slab.'

'Then why disappear from the mortuary?' I said.

'Because I overheard someone bribe the mortuary attendant for a private look at my body. So I just got up and walked out, while no one was looking, and came here. Because who would look for me in such a public place?'

'Had you warned Frank that you were going to fake your own death?' said Penny.

'Of course,' said Vincent, not even trying to hide his impatience at being interrupted. 'He knew I was an alien.'

'How?' said Penny.

'Because I told him, long ago,' said Vincent. 'He took it in his stride.'

'What was he to you?' said Penny.

'Frank was a good friend,' Vincent said slowly. 'He never asked questions, even though I knew he wanted to. I suppose it was inevitable that an alien passing for human would find much in common with a gay man passing as straight. We both understood about having to hide our true nature from those who would hurt us.'

'Ellie knew Frank was gay,' I said. 'And I got the impression a lot of other people in town knew.'

'As long as he never actually came out and said it, the town was prepared to overlook it,' said Vincent.

'I can't believe people here actually cared,' said Penny. 'Not in this day and age.'

'Norton Hedley is an old-fashioned town, in many ways,' said Vincent.

'How much did you tell Frank about what you really are?' I said.

'As much as I thought he could cope with. I showed him a few shape-changing tricks; he thought that was hilarious. But I didn't want to burden him with things he couldn't hope to understand. If I'd frightened him—'

'He might have given you up to the townspeople?' said Penny.

'He might not have wanted to be my friend any more,' said Vincent. He gave me a meaningful look. 'How much have you told her?'

'I barely remember anything about what I used to be,' I said. 'But . . . she's seen a few things.'

'And she's still with you?'

'She's my partner,' I said.

'Damn straight,' said Penny.

Vincent just shrugged.

'Didn't you ever feel the need for a partner?' I said.

'I have enjoyed being human,' said Vincent. 'But human beings are such fleeting things. We have the golden blood. We walk in eternity.'

'I know that,' I said. 'And so does Penny.'

'When you pass through the door, it will remake you into what you should be,' said Vincent. 'And then you will remember why gods should never love mortals.'

Penny looked at me, waiting for me to say I didn't want to go. I looked steadily at Vincent.

'Would you have taken Frank with you, if you could?' I said.

'I did think about it,' he said slowly. 'But the door would have had to change him so much, so that he could survive where we were going . . . And I don't think he could have coped.' He looked suddenly tired. 'I should never have left him here, alone and unprotected. But once I sensed you'd entered the wood, I had to try to warn you. It's a dangerous place for people like us.'

'Is it a genius loci?' I said.

'The wood stands directly above the door,' said Vincent. 'Centuries of proximity have changed the wood's nature. It has become psychoactive, digging into the minds of those who pass through it and reflecting what it finds there. Just as the door looks inside you, to work out what you need to be to survive where you're going.'

'If people change their shape when they go through,' said Penny, 'no wonder so few of them ever want to come back.'

Vincent ignored her, concentrating on me. 'I was on my way to the wood when Ellie died.'

'Who told you?' said Penny.

'No one told me,' said Vincent. 'I just knew. Live in this town long enough and you become attuned to it. The door didn't just change the wood.'

I remembered the crowd outside the hotel, with the same look in so many eyes.

'After Ellie died, I was worried the killer might be tracking down people I'd been close to,' said Vincent. 'To make them give up what they knew about me. I hurried back here to warn Frank not to talk to strangers, but he was already dead, without a mark on him. Just like Winston and Ellie.'

'Could our ancient enemy have come here?' I said.

'So . . . you do remember some things,' said Vincent.

'I ran into one of them, a few years back,' I said. 'I know they can possess people. But there's still so much I need to know . . . Why did our ship come to Earth? Was it because of the door? Do we still have a mission to finish here, before we can leave?'

Vincent looked at me with a terrible sad patience. 'I can't answer any of your questions, because you wouldn't understand the answers while you're still human. Come with me and let the door change you. And then all will become clear.'

'Don't listen to him, Ishmael,' Penny said urgently. 'I don't trust him!'

Vincent got to his feet. 'Now that Frank is dead, I have no reason to stay. Whoever killed him is still out there, searching for us, so I am going to the door, right now. With or without you, Ishmael.'

I looked at Penny. 'I need to see this door.'

'You're ready to walk away from a murder case, without even trying to stop the killer?' she said. 'Ishmael, this isn't like you.'

'You have no idea what he's really like,' said Vincent. 'Be grateful.'

'There are no clues and no suspects, unless it is the ancient enemy,' I said. 'And they could be anyone. This door could give me answers I've been looking for my whole life. I have to do this, Penny.'

'Will you be coming back?' she said. 'Or are you getting ready to run out on me? Like you did with so many others?'

'That isn't the plan,' I said.

'We've come this far together,' she said. 'You can't leave me behind now.'

'I have to.'

'Why? Because it's dangerous? You know I can look after myself.'

'This isn't human business any more,' I said. 'I can't be sure a human could survive where I'm going.'

'I'll risk it!'

'I won't.'

She looked at me steadily. 'If you walk out on me now, don't expect me to be here when you get back.'

'You'll be where you need to be,' I said. 'Trust me, Penny, the way I trust you . . . to do the right thing.'

I looked into her eyes until I was sure she understood. And then I turned away and followed Vincent out of the library.

ELEVEN
Who's Who
And What's What

The moment Vincent and I walked out of the library, Violet Silver was waiting for us. Standing slouched in her baggy clothes, smiling calmly in her usual drowsy manner, she might have been hanging around to greet old friends. But she wasn't, and all of us knew it. Interestingly, Violet didn't seem particularly surprised to discover that Vincent Smith was still very much among the living.

'Can I help you with something, Inspector?' I said politely.

'I allowed you and Ms Belcourt to leave the hotel, so I could follow you,' Violet said easily. 'You left far too many questions unanswered, Mr Jones.'

'What answers I have wouldn't help you,' I said.

'I get to decide that, not you.'

Vincent made a low aggrieved noise, and when I turned to look at him, he fixed me with a heavy stare.

'You didn't realize you were being followed?'

'Penny and I were concentrating on getting to Frank,' I said.

'I know you've been human a long time,' said Vincent, 'but I would have thought even you could manage to concentrate on more than one thing at a time.'

'Don't start,' I said. 'I'm more interested in why the inspector isn't freaking out big time at the sight of you, Mr Dead Man Walking.'

'Oh, she and I go way back,' said Vincent. 'She knows me better than most, and she's always been very hard to surprise. Isn't that right, Vi?'

'You never were as clever as you believed, Vince,' she said easily. 'Though I will admit, I would like to know why you're looking so much younger.'

'Death agrees with me,' said Vincent.

'Can you at least tell me why you're not stretched out on a slab in the mortuary?'

'I got bored, just lying around,' said Vincent.

'I examined you at your cottage, before they took you away,' said Violet. 'No pulse, no heartbeat, no breath . . . But I still couldn't bring myself to believe that you were actually dead.'

'I didn't know you cared, Vi,' said Vincent.

'I didn't,' said Violet. 'I just knew a setup when I saw one.' She looked him over with her heavy-lidded gaze, taking her time. 'I always had my suspicions that there was a lot more to you than met the eye. You always had so much . . . energy, for an older man.'

Vincent looked at me. 'She's talking about sex.'

'I got that,' I said.

'I never could get over how much you knew,' said Violet. 'About so many things. And no matter how weird it got here in town, you always took it in your stride. That's not normal – at least, not for someone who wasn't born here. But even though you were always ready to immerse yourself in the town's stranger aspects, you always felt like an outsider. As though there was something different about you, that you had to hide.'

'You have no idea,' said Vincent. 'Trust me.'

'That'll be the day,' said Violet.

'So,' I said, fixing Vincent with my own heavy stare, 'you and the inspector were an item?'

'It's a small town,' he said. 'You have to do something to pass the time when you're not working.'

'I thought you and Frank . . .'

'So did everyone,' said Vincent. 'Made for a great cover. Frank went along. He thought it was funny.'

'You said you never had a partner.'

'I didn't. It wasn't that kind of relationship.'

'It wasn't any kind of relationship,' said Violet. 'It was just sex.'

'I like sex,' said Vincent.

'How very human of you,' I said. 'But why go to such pains to keep this non-relationship a secret?'

'Because I couldn't afford to give hostages to fortune,' said Vincent.

'Same here,' said Violet.

'And no one in the town knew?' I said.

Violet shrugged. 'Norton Hedley has so many secrets that it wasn't difficult to hide one more.' She turned back to Vincent. 'I'm still waiting for an explanation as to why you're not lying toes up in the mortuary.'

'Then you'll just have to go on waiting,' said Vincent. 'Because an explanation wouldn't do you any good. What's happening now is beyond police work.'

'It is very definitely in everyone's best interests for you to stand aside and let us go, Inspector,' I said.

Violet stayed right where she was. 'No one is above the law.'

'Not even when they've been declared officially dead?' said Vincent.

She smiled briefly. 'Perhaps especially then. Don't try to out-weird me, Vince. This is Norton Hedley, where the strange stuff comes as standard.' She turned her speculative gaze on me. 'I knew there had to be some connection between you and Vince.'

'To be fair,' I said, 'I did tell you I came to this town specifically to meet him. What are you doing here, Inspector? Why aren't you pursuing the killer?'

'That's exactly what I am doing,' said Violet. 'You're responsible for all the deaths in Norton Hedley, Mr Jones. You and Ms Belcourt. It had to be the two of you because you're the only outsiders in this town.'

It took me a moment before I could say anything. 'That's it? We must have killed all those people because . . . we're not from around here?'

'To be fair,' said Vincent, 'you really aren't.'

I shot him a cold look. 'Definitely not helping, Vince.'

'You live long enough in this town, you become a part of it,' said Violet. 'I told you: there hasn't been a murder in Norton Hedley since 1928. We don't kill each other, because we're all so close it would be too much like killing ourselves.'

I remembered the crowd, with something else looking out from behind their eyes . . . and finally I understood.

'It's a group mind, isn't it?' I said. 'A gestalt, which only materializes in times of trouble – when the town believes it's under threat. That's why you can't be really local, unless you're born here.'

Vincent nodded. 'There was a reason I never fitted in. Apart from the obvious one, of course.'

'Don't think you can distract me,' said Violet, fixing me with a gaze that wasn't even a bit drowsy any more. 'You have no alibi for any of the murders.'

'I didn't know I was going to need one,' I said. 'If I had, I would have arranged something. I do have Penny to vouch for me.'

'But who vouches for her?' said Violet.

'And one of the supposed murder victims is standing right here beside me, very much alive.'

'Will Winston and Ellie be coming back to life as well?' said Violet. 'No? I didn't think so.'

Vincent sighed quietly, in a put-upon kind of way. 'We really don't have time for this, Vi.'

'Then make some,' said Violet. She studied me thoughtfully. 'Where is Ms Belcourt?' And then she looked quickly around, as though to make sure Penny wasn't sneaking up on her.

'Penny is in the library, with Frank,' I said. 'He's dead.'

Violet glared at me. 'You killed Frank? Damn you! I liked Frank.'

'They didn't kill him,' said Vincent. 'I found Frank lying dead by his desk when I came here to hide out. Ishmael and Penny only turned up afterwards.'

'Pardon me if I find it hard to believe anything you say, after you let all your friends believe you were dead,' said Violet. 'Why would you do something like that, Vince? Could it have something to do with your new and freakishly young appearance?'

'Do you like it?' said Vincent.

She shook her head. 'I was fine with you the way you were.'

Vincent looked at me. 'Even as a young woman, Vi always had serious daddy issues.'

'Did your new youth have to be paid for?' Violet said

harshly. 'Did innocent people have to die, so you could have a new life?'

Vincent smiled at me apologetically. 'This is what living in Norton Hedley does to you. They always go straight for the weirdest explanation.'

'People drop dead, without a mark on them, and here you are, looking like an advertisement for the fountain of youth,' said Violet. 'Pardon me if I can't help thinking there's a connection.'

I turned to Vincent. 'You know her best. Why is she so determined that everything has to be down to us?'

'Because we're outsiders,' said Vincent. 'In a town that has no room for such things.'

I nodded slowly. 'The underground door didn't just affect the nature of the wood, did it? It changed the townspeople as well.'

'When the original founders came here to build a town over the door, to conceal it from the world, that wasn't necessarily their idea,' said Vincent. 'The town needed people to protect it, from other people.'

'The door runs the town?'

'The people serve the door, as and when necessary. And in return they get a calm and peaceful life in a town that never changes.'

'Then why do so many people go missing?' I said.

'Not everyone born here belongs here,' said Vincent. 'There are always going to be some who don't fit the town's chosen parameters. They always end up searching for the door to the Other World, because they're different in some way, and they can tell the town doesn't want them. And the door is always happy to send them somewhere else, so they won't upset the balance. That's why no one local ever makes much of a fuss when one of their family members goes missing.'

Violet looked as if she wanted to put up a hand to attract our attention, like a child at school.

'What are you two talking about?'

'You've lived here too long, Vi,' said Vincent, not unkindly. 'You're so close that you can't see the wood for the trees.'

Violet pushed the thought aside and fixed him with a steady gaze. 'Why aren't you more upset that Frank is dead? He was your friend. More than I ever was.'

'You said that was what you wanted.'

'It was!'

'It was your idea we broke up,' Vincent said mildly.

'It was time.'

'Then why are you still so angry?'

'We are talking about Frank,' Violet said grimly.

'I will miss Frank,' said Vincent. 'But I never look back. You should know that.'

Violet turned her angry gaze on me. 'Did Frank have to die, so you could take his place?'

I was genuinely thrown for a moment. 'Where did that come from?'

'Is it really so unlikely?' said Violet. 'You came here with Ms Belcourt, but you're leaving with Vincent. So where is the poor girl now? Lying dead in the library, next to Frank?'

'Penny is fine,' I said. 'Go into the library and talk to her. And then you can go off in search of the real killer, who is still out there somewhere.'

'Well . . . you would say that, wouldn't you?' said Violet. 'I have no reason to trust you. Not least because wherever you go, there are bodies. You have questions to answer, Mr Jones.'

'I'm a bit busy, just at the moment,' I said.

'They all say that,' said Violet. 'Come along with me, Mr Jones. You're under arrest.'

'Do you have a weapon?' I said politely.

For the first time, Violet seemed taken aback, as she realized I had no intention of going quietly.

'Do *you* have a weapon?' she said challengingly.

I smiled. 'I don't need one.'

And something in the way I said that, or perhaps something in my smile, threw her again. She started to look to Vincent and then stopped herself, knowing she wouldn't find any support there. She met my gaze squarely.

'I can't just let you walk away. I'm the law in Norton Hedley.'

'No,' said Vincent. 'That's the door.'

'What door?' said Violet, her voice rising in spite of herself.

Vincent turned to me. 'We have to go. Deal with her.'

'I'm not going to kill her!' I said.

'I wasn't suggesting that you should,' said Vincent. 'You've spent too long working for those subterranean groups. Just subdue her and dump her in the library. Penny can let her go when this is all over.' He smiled at Violet. 'I can be sentimental, sometimes.'

'I may not have been born in the town,' Violet said steadily, 'but I've lived here long enough to feel a part of it. The townspeople will protect me.'

'No, they won't,' said Vincent.

The simple certainty in his voice gave Violet pause, and she looked at him narrowly.

'Why not?'

'Because the people serve the town, and the town serves the door,' said Vincent. 'And I have come to an accommodation with the door.'

It was my turn to look at him sharply. 'An accommodation? What exactly did you promise the door in return for sending you home?'

'The door is older than history,' said Vincent. 'It had become weak and hungry, so I fed it the ship. I understand the door found some of the tech very useful in making itself strong again.'

Violet looked very close to losing her temper. 'Someone had better start explaining things to me!'

'It's not anything you need to know,' Vincent said calmly. 'You go and do your job, Vi. Ishmael and I have places to go and things to be, and you can't be a part of it.'

Violet took a step forward, blocking our way.

'You are not going anywhere. I've already contacted my superiors, and reinforcements are on their way.'

'Alas, dear lady, I regret to inform you that the cavalry will not be appearing over the horizon in the nick of time, after all.'

Violet spun round to find Mr Whisper standing right behind her. I was caught off guard, too; he shouldn't have been able to get that close without my noticing. Vincent's face showed nothing at all, but he stood very still. Whisper bowed politely to Violet, before addressing her in his harsh murmur of a voice.

'There will be no reinforcements, Detective Inspector Silver. My people have talked to your people, and your request has been overruled. You are entirely on your own. And, I fear, very much out of your depth.'

Violet didn't appear worried or intimidated – just extremely wary.

'And who might you be?'

'I am Mr Whisper and I represent a higher authority. I am here to instruct you to go about your business and leave the three of us to ours.'

Violet looked at me, and I smiled.

'You wanted to know who I was working for. Meet Mr Whisper.'

Whisper nodded easily to Vincent. 'It is good to meet you at last, my dear sir. You look so much younger than your book covers.'

'I get that a lot,' said Vincent. He turned to me. 'Who is this, exactly?'

'I work for the Organization these days,' I said. 'He's one of their higher-ups.' I looked steadily at Whisper. 'What are you doing here?'

He smiled broadly. It wasn't any more convincing than usual, but I appreciated the effort.

'I am here to help, Mr Jones.' He turned his unwavering smile on Violet. 'Your superiors will be contacting you shortly to give you your instructions. Rest assured, neither of these people is the killer you have been searching for so diligently.'

Violet looked so furious I thought she might explode.

'I am the law in this town! People have died here, and it's my job to get some justice for them. So I am going to lock these two up until I can get someone to listen to me. And if you get in the way, Mr Whisper or whatever your name really is, you can join them!'

Whisper smiled calmly back at her.

'Feel free to argue with your superiors and fight for your principles, Inspector. See how far it gets you. I'm afraid that while you may be a big fish in this very small pond, we swim in the ocean. And we are used to fighting sharks.'

Violet looked at him steadily. 'Who are you? Security?'

'You're not cleared to know that,' said Whisper.

'Until someone I accept as an authority comes along and orders me to stand down,' said Violet, 'you can't make me do anything.'

'You're determined to be a nuisance, aren't you?' said Whisper. 'And this has ceased to be amusing.'

Before I could react, he hit her in the side of her face with vicious force, snapping her head right round. She had time to cry out once, and then he bludgeoned her to the ground with a second blow. She lay in a crumpled heap, her limbs twitching, as blood pooled around her head. Vincent gripped my arm fiercely, to hold me back. Whisper calmly adjusted his cuff, and smiled at the body as it stopped moving. For the first time, it looked like a real smile. I threw off Vincent's hand, knelt down beside Violet and checked her vital signs, and then looked up at Whisper.

'You killed her.'

'I made every effort to be civilized,' said Whisper. 'All she had to do was walk away.'

I rose to my feet, my hands clenched into fists. 'This isn't what the Organization does!'

'What do you know about the Organization, Mr Jones?' Whisper said calmly. 'You're just something we use, on occasion, to get things done.'

'Bullshit,' I said. 'You've gone rogue. And that stops here.'

'You really think you can stop me, Mr Jones?'

'You think I can't?'

'Don't, Ishmael,' Vincent said quietly. 'He's playing with you. There's more to this than you realize. More to him.'

Whisper smiled, and this time it looked like a shark showing off its teeth.

'Finally. I was beginning to think I'd have to spell it out for you.'

I looked at Vincent. 'Are you saying he's not working for the Organization?'

'I wouldn't know about that,' said Vincent. 'But perhaps the transformation machines gave me better eyes, because I knew from the first moment I saw him that Mr Whisper is no more human than you or I.'

'You mean he's like us?'

'No,' said Vincent. 'He's the enemy.'

Suddenly, a great many things made sense. Whisper laughed softly at the look on my face.

'I can't believe how easily you accepted I was who I said I was.'

'But . . . I checked with the Colonel!' I said. 'He confirmed you were high up in the Organization!'

'Oh, Mr Whisper is . . . but he hasn't been in the driving seat for some time now. These days, I wear him like a glove. My people discovered the AI imprisoned under Harrow House, calling out so piteously to those with ears to hear it, and then we used it as bait, so I could introduce myself to you and set the ball rolling. We knew there was something of great significance in this town, and it didn't take much to persuade you to authorize an investigation. Unfortunately, they didn't find what we were looking for, so I followed you here to see what you could uncover. And you have been extremely helpful.'

He turned his cold smile on Vincent. 'So your ship is no more? A pity. I'm sure we could have made good use of your people's secrets. But the door . . . That is so much more than we were expecting.'

'How did you find out about that?' said Vincent.

'People will talk,' said Whisper. 'They can't help themselves, once we inhabit them. All we need now is the exact location of the door, and you will give us that. With a door to every-where at our command, no one will be safe from us.'

'The door answers to no one,' said Vincent.

'It will do as it's told once my people take possession of it,' said Whisper. 'We know all there is to know when it comes to possession.'

'Why did your people come here?' I said. 'Why bring our war to Earth?'

'In the end, it all comes down to hate,' said Whisper. 'None of us will ever rest as long as one of you still lives.'

'That makes no sense at all,' I said.

'You've spent too long among humans,' said Whisper.

'What are you going to do now that you've found us?' I said. 'Try to kill us?'

'There was a time when I would have enjoyed taking you in for dissection and savoured your screams,' said Whisper. 'But why waste such useful insiders? I am large, I contain multitudes – more than enough to fill you both up to the brim and set you working for us. Of course, when I say *you*, what's left of you will be trapped deep inside, screaming endlessly in horror at what we make your bodies do, but that's just a bonus.'

'Did you kill Winston, and Ellie, and Frank?' I said.

'Unfortunately, no. I've been far too busy,' said Whisper. 'But now it's time to take possession of my new assets.'

He fixed Vincent with his gaze, and just like that he was frozen in place. Vincent's eyes stared wildly as he struggled to move and found he couldn't. I went for Whisper, calling on all my inhuman strength and speed, but his gaze switched to mine and I slammed to a halt, caught in mid-step. I looked into Whisper's eyes and saw something awful glaring back at me. A thing of horror and terrible intent, rising up from the depths of something that only looked human. I threw all my will against it, and its hold on me wavered. I had spent so much of my life struggling to be human, and there were two minds inside me. My other self moved forward, from out of the shadows at the back of my mind, to stand alongside me . . . And faced with two minds to conquer, Whisper's will divided and shattered against our defiance. We broke free.

Whisper staggered backwards. Vincent made a low pained noise, shaking his head hard to clear it.

'How did you do that?'

'Stubbornness,' I said. I smiled at Whisper. 'Now what are you going to do?'

He snarled at me, and his hand dived inside his jacket for a weapon. I braced myself to jump him, knowing I'd never reach him in time. And that was when the Colonel stepped calmly out of a side street and shot Whisper in the face with a weapon made from glowing crystal. Something alien burst out of Whisper's body: a form with no shape, or at least nothing the human mind could hope to comprehend. Like a colour from the wrong side of the rainbow, the alien thing that had been possessing Mr Whisper coiled and writhed on the air, slowly dispersing, until every last bit of it was gone. Whisper's body collapsed and lay motionless on the ground, breathing slowly and emptily.

'Nice shot,' I said to the Colonel. Because I had to say something.

'Military training,' he said. 'You never forget how.'

Vincent gave me a hard look as the Colonel put his weapon away.

'This is my contact man with the Organization,' I said. 'And I have no idea what's going on here.'

'Sorry I had to wait till the last moment,' said the Colonel. 'But I needed to know what its plans were.'

I glared at him. 'Where did you come from?'

'I arrived in Norton Hedley before you did,' said the Colonel. 'It was easy enough for me to stay hidden in the shadows, with you doing so much to stand out and be noticed. The Organization has had its suspicions about Whisper for some time.'

'You knew an alien was possessing one of our people?'

'We knew we'd been infiltrated by an outside agent,' said the Colonel. 'We just weren't sure who they were hiding inside. We also knew about you, Mr Jones.'

I didn't have to ask what he knew.

'What is the Organization, really?' I said.

'On the surface, just what it appears to be,' said the Colonel. 'Underneath, it's an underground railway for aliens passing as human, who need help to get home. There are more strange visitors walking around in this world than you realize.'

'Why didn't you offer me a way home?' I said.

'Because you weren't ready to commit yourself.'

'Are you an alien?' I asked bluntly.

'Of course not,' said the Colonel. 'The Organization is a human group, supporting aliens.'

'Why would you do that?' said Vincent.

'Because it's in everyone's best interests,' said the Colonel. 'Now then, off you go about your business, and I'll take care of Mr Whisper and Inspector Silver. The clean-up crew are already on their way.'

'Oh, Violet isn't dead,' I said. 'I just told Whisper that so he'd leave her alone. Look after her, Colonel. She only tried to do her duty.'

'Of course,' said the Colonel.

'Are you sure that thing inside Whisper was the only one of its kind here?' I said. 'They could have possessed any number of people.'

'Mr Nemo has already checked out the town, from a distance,' the Colonel said calmly. 'And he assures me the only other alien presences are you and Mr Smith. And the door, of course.'

'You know about that, as well?' said Vincent.

'Of course,' said the Colonel.

'And the alien war?' I said.

'We know what we need to know,' said the Colonel.

'Is there anything you can do for the real Whisper?' I said, gesturing at the unmoving body. 'He might still be in there, somewhere.'

'I'll have Mr Nemo take a quick look inside his head,' said the Colonel. 'Just in case there's any trace of the original still hanging around.'

I looked at him steadily. 'Do you know who the killer is?'

'Haven't a clue,' said the Colonel. 'Identifying killers has always been your province, not mine.'

'All right,' I said. 'Leave it to me.'

TWELVE

Not out of the Woods Yet

Afternoon was shading into evening, and the light was going out of the day, as Vincent and I walked on through the town. Shadows crept in from every side, and the antiquated buildings took on a dark and brooding aspect. After a while, it occurred to me that the streets had gone back to being empty and quiet again. No traffic, no pedestrians, not even a twitching curtain at a window. I turned to Vincent.

'Where is everybody? I was half expecting the town gestalt to show up and escort us to wherever it is we're going.'

'The town isn't interested any more,' said Vincent. 'The door has marked us for its own.'

'So the door has put down a welcome mat?'

'I don't know that I'd go that far,' said Vincent.

I gave him my best hard look. 'I thought you'd come to an accommodation with the door?'

'I have,' said Vincent. 'But a lot has changed since you showed up.'

'I don't see any reason to say that as if it's my fault.'

He shrugged. 'Violet had a point. People really didn't start dropping dead until you came to town.'

'I know who the murderer is,' I said.

Vincent looked at me sharply. 'You do?'

'There's only one person it could be. But that will have to wait until our business is finished.'

'You won't be coming back,' said Vincent. 'Not after you've seen what the door can do for you.'

I stared straight ahead. 'Where exactly are we going?'

'To the wood.'

He gestured ahead, to where the street came to an end in

a gathering of dark trees and darker shadows, and a sense of things concealed.

'Is there any part of this town that the wood isn't sneaking up on?' I said.

'The wood exists to serve the door,' said Vincent.

'Doesn't everything around here?'

Vincent surprised me by taking my question seriously. 'It's hard to tell. Norton Hedley didn't just happen; it was created to protect and preserve the door.'

'Then why is so much of the town seriously weird?'

'Because its creator is even less human than we are.'

I scowled at the looming trees. 'Is there any other way to get to the door?'

'Not really, no. Why are you looking at the wood like that?'

'Because I know how dark it gets in there.'

'Nothing to worry about,' Vincent said briskly. 'Not now we have the door's protection.'

'If the town was built over the door,' I said thoughtfully, 'why do we have to go into the wood to access it?'

'Because the wood is the halfway point between the world of the town and the world of the door.'

'Why?' I said bluntly.

'Because that's the way the door wanted it,' said Vincent, just as bluntly.

When we finally reached the trees, they didn't look at all as I remembered. Everything seemed subtly blurred and out of focus, as though my mind couldn't decide what it was supposed to be seeing. Or perhaps the wood was having trouble deciding which face it wanted to show me.

I stood at the edge and stared hard at the trees, until one by one they snapped into sharp focus, although the shadows that held them together were still as dark as a starless night. When I finally strode forward into the wood, with Vincent right behind me, it was like walking into a dream . . . into a place where all the rules were different, and reality was a sometime thing.

The darkness fell upon us with almost indecent haste, leaving the trees little more than dim shapes. The wood was

silent as a tomb, and about as welcoming. It felt as though
the trees were just waiting for me to make a mistake, so they
could take advantage. I was in enemy territory, and the
territory was the enemy.

There was no path this time, not even a beaten trail, and
where my feet came down on the dark earth, blood seeped up
to fill my footprints. The trees didn't look like trees any
more – just tall dark shapes, twisted and deformed, full of
malice and bad intent. Their branches stretched out hungrily,
writhing and twitching, but somehow always pulled back at
the last moment rather than touch me or Vincent.

Penny said walking in the wood reminded her of the wild
woods in fairy stories, but this felt more like the dark and
primordial forests of the older tales, which existed long
before the more family-friendly versions appeared. Stories
where lost children never made it out alive, the witch gnawed
on undersized bones, and the wolf licked blood from his
teeth. In a wood like this, death and horror would always be
a part of the story.

Vincent raised his voice cheerfully, apparently entirely unaf-
fected by his surroundings.

'Two aliens in human form, walking through a psychoactive wood fashioned from the needs of a door older than
human civilization . . . Who knows what it will show us?
The wood must be lost for choices, with all the recesses of
our minds to draw on.'

'Is everything we see in here just an illusion?' I said. 'Or
does the wood change physically, to reflect our thoughts?'

'Mostly, the wood deals in dreams and delusions,' said
Vincent. 'Whatever it takes, to distract people or drive them
away from the door. But the wood does have its own reality.
Things can get pretty weird.'

'If the door is so eager to see us,' I said carefully, 'why
does the wood feel so angry?'

'I don't know,' said Vincent. 'Did you do something to
upset it the last time you were here?'

'I might have,' I said. 'You keep talking about the wood
as though it has a mind of its own. Does it?'

Vincent shrugged. 'Who knows? After so many years of

being so many things, there's no way of telling what the wood has made of itself.'

'You could say the same about Norton Hedley,' I said.

'No,' said Vincent. 'The town and its people can't change too much, or the world would notice. And the door doesn't want that. Most of the time, the townspeople are perfectly normal. I doubt they even remember what they do when the town has need of them.'

'I really don't like the idea of the townspeople being used as pawns,' I said. 'Controlled by an alien force. That sounds far too much like our ancient enemy.'

'The gestalt only emerges in cases of real emergency,' Vincent said patiently. 'And in return, the townspeople have the door's protection.'

'What do they need protecting from?' I said.

'The rest of the world,' said Vincent. 'You must have noticed how peaceful Norton Hedley is. The perfect small country town, untouched by all the evils of the modern age. Admittedly, it is rather old-fashioned in some ways, particularly in its attitude to people who are different.'

'Like Frank?'

Vincent didn't look at me. 'The template the door used to shape the town's population was derived from the source material it had to work with, back in the sixth century. But things are changing. Mostly due to the internet. I'm not actually sure why the door allowed that. Perhaps it was lonely.'

'Is the door alive and aware?' I said.

'I'm not sure such terms mean anything when applied to something so far beyond our understanding,' said Vincent. 'All that matters is that it's something we can bargain with.'

And then he stopped, and I stopped with him. All around us, the trees' branches were swaying menacingly, as though moved by a stubborn malice . . . but I couldn't see anything worrying enough to justify the frown on Vincent's face.

'What's wrong?' I said.

'I keep getting this feeling that we're being followed,' he said quietly.

'It's just the wood,' I said.

Vincent stared back the way we'd come, straining his eyes against the deepening gloom. 'Are you sure?'

'I've been doing the secret agent thing a long time,' I said. 'I've learned to trust my instincts. If anyone from the town had followed us in, I'd know. Unless . . . Are there things living in this wood that you haven't seen fit to mention?'

'The wood does like to play games with people's heads,' said Vincent. 'Keep going. We need to get to the door before it has time to think and change its mind.'

'I thought you'd made a deal with it?' I said as we set off again, forcing our way between tightly packed trees and stepping over curling roots that had burst up through the earth.

'Sacrificing the ship bought me some good will,' said Vincent. 'But I don't know how long that will last.'

'And you think we should trust our lives to something that fickle?' I said.

'Keep your voice down!' hissed Vincent. 'It can hear us . . .'

'You are really not selling this door to me.'

'With the ship gone, the door is our only way home. You do want to go home, don't you?'

'I'm still thinking.'

'What's there to think about?' said Vincent.

'If you don't know,' I said, 'I can't explain it to you.'

We walked on for some time, without getting anywhere. The trees seemed to lurch forward every time I took my eyes off them, and the clawed fingers on the reaching branches only just fell short of our faces. It seemed to me that the gloom was getting darker.

'How big is this wood?' I said finally.

'As big as it needs to be,' said Vincent.

'Is it always this . . . threatening?'

'Not usually, no.' Vincent looked around uncertainly. 'The wood only reflects what we bring to it. The trees shouldn't be this bad, unless something really dangerous has entered the wood.' He turned abruptly to look at me. 'Do you have some plan in mind that you are keeping from me, Ishmael?'

A fleeting movement up ahead caught my eye. I lowered my voice.

'Don't look now, but we are definitely not alone. Is there something I should know, Vincent?'

'There are people who come into the wood and never get to leave,' Vincent said reluctantly.

'Are you saying the wood has the power to stop them?'

'If the wood believes in something long enough, it becomes real,' said Vincent. 'Or real enough to imprison anyone who might pose a threat to the door. Some of these prisoners are supposed to have been here a really long time.'

'What kind of people are we talking about?' I said.

'Tourists with too vivid an imagination, who became lost in their own nightmares. Journalists who got too close to the truth. People who brought too much darkness into the wood with them . . . The wood was given power to protect the door from outside threats, and now and again people break under the pressure of its regard. And sometimes . . . I think the wood just likes to play with its prey.'

'I don't suppose you're carrying any kind of weapon?'

'No,' said Vincent. 'How about you, Mr Very Secret Agent?'

'I don't normally need one,' I said.

A dark figure flitted between the trees like a drifting thought, come and gone so quickly I wasn't even sure what I'd seen. It might have been human once. I grabbed hold of a nearby branch and broke it off to use as a weapon, and the dark figure suddenly reared up before us, blocking our way. Half hidden in the gloom, it looked like something that had lived in the wood so long it had taken on the aspect of the trees. Its once human form was twisted and crooked, and covered in gnarled bark. The clawed hands were bunches of twigs, the face was a cracked and splintered mask, and its eyes were patches of blood-red moss. It didn't stand like a man. Perhaps because it had forgotten how.

I glanced at Vincent, but he had no advice to offer, so I made myself smile pleasantly at the figure.

'Hello? Can we help you?'

'You don't belong here,' said the tree man in a dry and scratchy voice. 'Get out, or I'll hurt you. The wood will make me hurt you.'

'Why threaten us?' I said. 'We don't mean any harm.'

The figure paused uncertainly, as though it had been ready to face anything except calm and reasonable words.

'Who are you?' I said. 'Can you tell us your name?'

The wooden head tilted to one side, perhaps because its bark-covered face could no longer exhibit emotions.

'I forgot my name long ago,' it said slowly. 'I had to. It hurt too much to remember the life I used to have. Before the trees closed in around me and wouldn't let me out.'

I glared at Vincent. 'This is what the door does to people who try to find it?'

'Not the door,' said Vincent. 'The wood.'

'But the wood serves the door!'

'Sometimes . . . the door sleeps.'

'We can't leave him here, like this,' I said flatly.

'There's nothing we can do.'

'We can talk to the door!'

'Do you really want to risk upsetting it and throw away our one chance to get off this world?'

'You have to get out of the wood!' said the tree man. 'Or the wood will make me kill you. Its thoughts are so much stronger than mine. I drown in them.'

'You can't touch us,' Vincent said firmly. 'We're here because this is what the door wants.'

'Death and murder have come into the wood,' said the tree man. 'The door must be protected.'

Vincent looked at me. 'Is he talking about you?'

I looked at the heavy branch in my hand, threw it away and smiled reassuringly at the tree man.

'You've been here too long,' I said. 'Come with me. I'll take you to the boundary.'

The tree man took a hesitant step forward and then stopped. 'How can I leave? Look what the wood has done to me.'

'Maybe you'll change back,' I said. 'When it no longer has a hold over you.'

'The wood isn't known for its quality of mercy,' said the tree man. 'Anyway, after being away for so long, would I even recognize the world out there?' The bark-covered shoulders heaved suddenly, as though trying to remember how to cry. 'I can't go back, but I can't stand to be like this any longer.'

'You poor bastard,' I said. 'Come here.'

I stepped forward, took the tree man in my arms and hugged him as best I could. He cracked and splintered and fell away, until there was nothing left of him to hold. I brushed the last few flakes off my clothes and looked at Vincent.

'Is he free now?'

'Whatever part of him was trapped here,' said Vincent.

'How many other altered people are there in this wood?'

'You're assuming he was real,' said Vincent.

'Answer the question!'

'The wood serves the door,' Vincent said steadily. 'And the door . . . takes the long view. We have to assume that things are the way they are for a reason.'

'I'm going to have words with this door,' I said.

'Ishmael, you can't upset it! The door is our only hope!'

'Watch me.'

I moved on, and after a moment Vincent came after me. The trees were packed so close together now that I had to turn sideways to edge past them, peering into the gloom ahead for some sign of where we were going. I could feel a new tension on the air, though I wasn't sure whether that came from the wood or from Vincent.

'Don't you want to go home?' he said finally.

'This world is my home.'

'You can't want to stay on Earth! We don't belong here!'

'You stayed in Norton Hedley long enough,' I said.

'The longer I stayed, the more I got into the habit of being a man,' said Vincent. 'But now you're here, I've started to remember things. We have to go back; we're needed.'

'Are you about to tell me there's a war going on, out among the stars, and we have duties and responsibilities?'

'Yes!' said Vincent.

'I know and I don't care,' I said. 'That's who I used to be. I have duties and responsibilities here now.'

Vincent started to say something and then stopped.

'Penny means a lot to you, doesn't she?'

'She's my partner,' I said.

'But you left her behind.'

'I trust her to do the right thing,' I said steadily.

'It's a mistake to get attached to people,' said Vincent. 'They don't last. I made a good life here, but I always knew I was only passing through.'

'Tell me about the door,' I said, in a tone that made it clear we were changing the subject.

'What's there to tell?' said Vincent.

'How about *everything*?'

'It's the door to anywhere,' said Vincent. 'Step through and you can be on any world you want. And in whatever shape or form you need to be to survive there.'

'Did our ship come here to look for this door?' I said.

'No,' said Vincent. 'Our predecessors located it. We wanted to find out what happened to the ones who built it.'

'Why is that so important?'

'We need allies in our war. Or at least we did. Who knows what's happened in all the time we've been stranded here.'

'I think we can safely assume the war is still going on,' I said. 'Or the alien inside Mr Whisper wouldn't have come after us.'

'You must know they'll never stop coming after you, if you stay.'

I looked at him. 'How much do you remember of your life before you were human?'

Vincent shrugged uncomfortably. 'Only what my human mind can cope with.'

'Have you ever seen your original self?' I said. 'In a mirror or a dream?'

'No,' said Vincent. 'Have you?'

'Sometimes,' I said.

'What was it like?'

'Alien,' I said. 'Monstrous.'

'To your eyes,' said Vincent. 'Were you able to talk?'

'That might be overstating the case,' I said. 'We have agreed to coexist. How did you find the door?'

Vincent brightened; he did so like to tell his stories.

'Once I began my research into why so many people had gone missing, I couldn't believe how many there were. I started questioning the local families who'd lost someone, but most didn't want to talk about it. And that's when I got my first glimpse of the gestalt in action, as the town took steps to shut me down.

'I continued my research, in private, and that led me to stories about a door to the Other World. A familiar enough legend, about the perils involved in visiting fairies under the hill. Except there were clues in the local stories about how to find this door. And then I discovered that others had followed these clues before me, gone off in search of the door and never returned.

'Did they find this door and go through it? I had to know. The clues led me to the wood; the first time I walked through the trees, the door reached out to me. And showed me how to find it.'

'Why would it do that?' I said.

'Because it recognized what I used to be.'

I nodded slowly. 'How much further do we have to go?'

'Oh, we're already there,' said Vincent. 'We were there the moment we entered the wood.'

I stopped and looked at him sharply.

'We haven't really been going anywhere,' Vincent said cheerfully. 'We've just been presenting ourselves, so the door could study you from a distance and decide whether to grant you an audience.'

'Then why is it taking so long?' I said loudly.

Vincent winced. 'Please, Ishmael, you have to be careful how you talk to the door. Be polite or we'll never get to go home.'

'I don't really do polite.'

'Oh, God. We're doomed.'

A blaze of light flared up, pushing back the dark, before dying down into a warm, comfortable glow from dozens of windows in a huge old mansion house. A great sprawling structure that I recognized immediately, with its arched gables and gargoyles at every corner. The trees surrounded the house, pressing up against its walls and windows, and silhouetted against the light like so many protective guards. As though the house had been there first and the wood grew up around it.

'That's Murdstone Manse,' I said. 'What has that got to do with the door?'

'It *is* the door,' said Vincent.

'It's inside the house?'

'What did you expect? A door standing on its own in the middle of a clearing? This house is as old as the town, and has known many forms down the years. The name Murdstone comes from the family who used to live in it. Before and after that, the house's true name was Heaven's Way.'

I looked at the house and the house looked back, giving nothing away.

'All right,' I said. 'What do we do now?'

'Walk through the front door and make ourselves known to what dwells there.'

'Local lore has it that the townspeople got together and burned the house down,' I said carefully. 'And for good reason.'

'The house wasn't the problem,' Vincent said patiently. 'The family who used to live in it were supposed to protect the house and preserve the door. And so they did, for many generations. But the house was old, even then, and it slept a lot. The family got greedy and restricted access to the door, in return for money and power. And then they started preying on the town, abducting the innocent and using them for their pleasure. So the townspeople got together and set the exterior of the house alight, to get its attention.

'The house woke up, and it woke up angry. It put out the flames with a thought, conversed with the gestalt, and forced every member of the Murdstone family through the door. Don't ask where it sent them, if you like sleeping. After that, the house decided to do without a resident family and removed itself from the town.'

'Why does it keep reappearing in different places?' I said.

'I think that sometimes it dreams of the town.'

'Why was the door put here in the first place?' I said.

'The Earth stands at a cosmic crossroads,' said Vincent. 'Where intergalactic ley lines come together, as they traverse the long night.' He smiled. 'Frank would have loved that . . .'

'How do you know all this?'

'Because the house told me. Why are you still standing there? Isn't this what you came all this way to see?'

'What's to stop the house from disappearing again?'

'We're expected.'

Some of the trees had fallen back when I wasn't looking, to allow me clear passage. I walked cautiously forward to stand before the front door. There didn't seem to be any bell or knocker, but when I reached out a hand to knock, the door swung silently back before me. Beyond it lay a great open lobby, illuminated by hundreds of candles. I raised my chin and walked through the open doorway as though I had a gilt-edged invitation in my pocket.

I have experience with big old houses.

Two suits of medieval armour stood at the foot of a massive stairway, as though they'd been set there to stand guard. They were immersed in thick swirls and mats of cobwebs, as though cocooned by generations of industrious spiders. They didn't look as if they'd been disturbed in ages. I couldn't see any more cobwebs in the lobby. All the antique furnishings and wood-panelled walls gleamed richly, as though they'd just been polished. The marble floor had been laid out in a chequerboard pattern, and there was no sign that anyone had walked on it in ages. I heard Vincent come in behind me, and then the door quietly shut itself behind us.

'How much of this is real, and how much is in my head?' I said quietly.

'Hard to tell,' said Vincent. 'This isn't what the house looked like the last time I was here. I'm guessing a lot of this is coming from your subconscious – what you expected to find here.'

'I thought the door was supposed to be deep underground?'

'It is. The door is the house, remember? When we entered the house, we left the wood behind and travelled to where the door is. We are deep under the wood now, and far from the world you know. So behave yourself. This is a place of myths and marvels, and we are very much the poor relations.'

'Speak for yourself,' I said.

Vincent sighed resignedly. 'Go ahead; introduce yourself.'

'Who to?'

'The house, of course.'

I raised my voice to address the empty lobby. 'Hello! My name is Ishmael Jones. I'm here about a door.'

And then I fell back a step, as the armoured knights slowly drew themselves up to their full height and the cobwebs tore and fell away. The knights flexed their steel arms, the bulky joints rasping loudly from lack of use. The featureless helmets turned as one, to focus on me.

'Keep your distance,' they said, in the same deep echoing voice. 'Know your place.'

'Knock it off,' I said. 'I'm expected.'

The knights drew their swords in one swift movement and stepped forward to block my way. The long steel blades gleamed viciously in the candlelight.

'I told you!' said Vincent, falling back as far as he could. 'You can't talk to the door like that!'

'Show some backbone,' I said.

And then I surged forward so quickly the knights in armour couldn't move fast enough to stop me. Their swords swept round in a deadly arc, but I ducked under them and kicked each knight hard in the side of the knee. They fell forward, overbalanced by the weight of their armour, and crashed down on to their hands and knees. I grabbed the nearest steel helmet and pulled it off; there was no one inside. The helmet vanished from my hands and, just like that, both knights had disappeared. I studied the space where they'd been suspiciously, then raised my voice again.

'I don't take any shit from my subconscious.'

'How very wise of you, sir.'

I looked up to see a large, dignified gentleman descending the stairs, dressed in an old-fashioned butler's outfit in severe black and white. He could have been any age; he had a straight back and a stern face with huge side-whiskers, although his eyes seemed surprisingly kind. He came to a halt before me at the foot of the stairs and waited patiently as I looked him over.

'Why are you dressed as a butler?' I said finally.

'It's your subconscious, sir. This is how you perceive me and my function.'

'What was the point of the two bouncers in armour?'

'Don't mind the watchdogs, sir; I think they just get a bit bored, waiting to be put to use.'

'And who exactly might you be?' I said, as politely as I could manage.

'I am the caretaker, sir. An interface with the house's AI, so you don't have to talk to thin air. That always upsets people. Would you care for some tea?'

'Not right now, thank you,' I said. 'But I would like some questions answered.'

'Ask away, sir.'

'Why is this house called Heaven's Way?'

'Because this is the way to the heavens, and all that they contain,' said the caretaker. 'The house exists to contain and preserve the door to everywhere. Holding it in trust, for when humanity has grown worthy of it. And then all of you will be free to walk among the stars.'

'Why do you need the townspeople and their gestalt?'

'Because I'm old, sir, and sleep a lot. They protect me, when I can't.'

The caretaker's voice was calm, wise and reassuring, like a kindly old uncle taking the time to answer some everyday question.

'And the people who aren't allowed to be a part of the gestalt, because they're different?'

'I offer a way out to all who feel they don't belong where they are.'

'I found someone in the wood,' I said. 'He'd been horribly altered by what he found there. How many people have been hurt, just trying to get to your door?'

'The tree man was no more real than the knights, or me,' said the caretaker. 'I'm afraid it's all just your human mind, attempting to interpret a complicated situation. Anyone who needs to use the door will always find me waiting here, to assist them.'

'I notice you've stopped calling me sir.'

'I do apologize, sir. Please continue.'

'What happened to the ones who made you?' I said.

'Long gone, sir,' said the caretaker. 'I wait for them to return.'

'But what if they don't?' I said. 'You have been here for a very long time.'

'I can wait,' said the caretaker. 'Forever, if need be. I was made to last. Now, where do you wish to go, sir?'

'We want to go home,' said Vincent, moving in beside me. 'To the world we came from.'

'Ah, yes,' said the caretaker. 'I know it well.'

He gestured, and a door was standing right next to us, alone and unsupported. It swung back to reveal a beach of stones that shone like diamonds. Churning and seething, they swirled in complex patterns. The ocean beyond the shore was a deep purple, its mountainous waves rising up high as skyscrapers, only to fall slowly back, more like some impossibly thick syrup than water. Long waves pounded the shore like a roll of cannon fire. Strange lights flared in the depths, like phosphorescent stars, and huge shapes moved ponderously among them.

A massive cliff face stared across the waters, its sickly grey surface shot through with pulsing veins. It bulged out, here and there, like rotting fruit or fruiting bodies. At the top of the cliff stood a huge artificial structure, composed of brightly shining metal plates, that was constantly changing its shape.

And all of this against a bottle-green sky, under a fierce white sun. Three small moons, their surfaces wrinkled like evil faces, shot across the cloudless sky as though in hot pursuit of each other. Wafting through the door came all the scents of home: poisoned meat and rotting metal, burned bones and the perfumes of corrupt flowers.

'Home is where the heart is,' said Vincent, smiling.

'I have seen this before,' I said. 'Down a black hole, in Brassknocker Hill. One of our own kind used this scene to tempt me to come home. I didn't want it then, and I don't want it now.'

'I could force you through the door,' said Vincent. 'Once you were your old self again, you'd understand why it was necessary.'

'You could try,' I said, and Vincent looked away.

The door closed itself, and the caretaker smiled on me benignly. 'How else can I be of service, sir?'

'Tell me what happened to all the people who passed through you,' I said.

'They went wherever they thought they could be happy, sir,' said the caretaker. 'To whatever destinations their souls yearned for. Somewhere they could finally fit in.'

'Were they still human when they got there?' I said.

'What makes you think they wanted to be?' said the caretaker.

'But they could return?' I said. 'If they wanted to?'

'Of course, sir,' said the caretaker. 'But who would want to leave paradise?'

The door opened again, to show me fairy-tale castles with jutting towers and furling flags, and futuristic cities with brightly shining buildings soaring up into the skies. Endless green gardens, where people wandered in happy ignorance of the burdens of civilization, and neon-lit streets where the party never ended and no one ever had to go home. Men and women swimming in oceans made of curling mists, or climbing mountains whose peaks brushed against the stars. All the dreams that ever were, and everything else under the suns. The door closed itself again and waited.

I looked at Vincent. 'The door to everywhere; I get the attraction. But what did our people find so urgent about it that they had to risk being shot down to come here?'

'We were hoping to make contact with potential allies from the other side of the door,' said Vincent. 'We've been fighting the war too long, and I think we might be losing.'

'You go through if you want,' I said. 'I'm not going anywhere.'

'Our people need you!' said Vincent.

'How could one more of you make any difference?' I said. 'This world needs me. I serve a function here. I solve mysteries and find murderers.'

'You could be so much more.'

'I'm content to be who I am.' And then I stopped as a thought struck me. 'What kind of allies were you looking for?'

'Powerful ones,' said Vincent.

'Did it never occur to you that you might catch the attention of something far worse than the ancient enemy?'

Vincent looked at the caretaker.

'It's always possible,' said the caretaker. 'The door opens from both sides. That's why there have been so many weird sightings in and around Norton Hedley. Just things that slipped through when I wasn't looking.'

'How is that even possible?' I said.

'Shit happens, sir,' said the caretaker. 'If you don't want to go home, perhaps I can tempt you with other places you might care to visit.'

The door opened again to show me a changing kaleido-scope of worlds. Islands floating in the sky, above organic landscapes that heaved and sighed. Mountains that sang and forests that danced, machine cities where the lights never went out as they worked endlessly to unknowable purposes . . . Giants whose tread shook the earth, and angels who shone like living suns. And then the interior of the door was suddenly a mirror, showing me my own stunned reflection. Which in turn gave way to a face I'd seen before. My previous self, before I was me. Alien, inhuman and monstrous beyond bearing. The other side of my face. It spoke to me, in slow solemn words that detonated inside my head.

'You could leave this world if you wanted.'

'The Earth is my home,' I said, 'if you'll let me stay.'

'I can wait,' said the alien.

'Why are you talking to me now?' I said.

'The door could help you remember everything. If you wanted.'

I thought about it and smiled. 'I can wait.'

My other self disappeared, and the door swung slowly shut. I turned to Vincent.

'So that's what I really look like,' he said.

'You still want to go back and be that?' I said.

Vincent smiled briefly. 'I never did feel easy in my own skin. I think it's time to change into someone more comfort-able. Any last message for the folks back home?'

'Tell them . . . they'll see me when they see me,' I said.

'And not to wait up. But before you go, we have some unfin-
ished business. A murderer to be brought to justice.'

Vincent frowned. 'Yes . . . I don't like the idea of leaving
with my friends' killer still unpunished.'

'Then this is your lucky day,' I said. 'Because they've come
to see you off. Isn't that right, Lucy?'

I turned around and there she was, grinning all over her
face as she pointed an alien weapon at us.

'How did she get in?' said Vincent.

'The front door was open,' said Lucy.

'I thought she was with you,' said the caretaker.

'This is the Black Heir field agent Lucy Parker,' I said to
Vincent. 'She's the one who followed us through the wood.'

Vincent looked at me sharply. 'I told you I heard someone!'

'It was all I could do to keep you from scaring her off,' I
said. 'I wanted her to join us here, for judgement.'

'That's why the wood was so dark,' said Vincent. 'It wasn't
responding to us; it was reacting to her!'

'What are you talking about?' said Lucy.

'You didn't see any strange things in the wood?' I said.

'Of course not; it was just trees.'

'Field agents like you always focus on the job at hand,'
I said. I nodded at the ugly weapon Lucy was holding. 'I
found something very like that in a crashed alien ship when
I worked for Black Heir. A weapon that kills without leaving
any trace. Once I remembered that, I knew the killer had to
be from Black Heir, and you were the only agent in town. I'm
sure I destroyed that weapon. How did you . . .?'

'It wasn't the first ship of its kind to crash,' said Lucy.
'There was bound to be another.'

'And how did you get your hands on that particular
weapon?' I said.

'How do you think?' said Lucy, grinning happily.

'You stole it.'

'Exactly!' And then the smile vanished, and she scowled
fiercely at me. 'How did you know I was following you? I'm
a trained field agent!'

'You're used to following people,' I said. 'I'm used to being
followed.'

'Well, that's all over now,' said Lucy.

Vincent started forward, and Lucy immediately covered him with the weapon. He stopped and stared at her coldly.

'You killed my friends. Frank, and Ellie, and Winston.'

'She's been very busy,' I said. 'Following her own agenda. I let her catch up with us so we could question her.'

'Shut up!' said Lucy. 'Look at you, still trying to act like you're in charge . . . I have the weapon, so that puts me in the driver's seat.' She glanced at the door, standing all on its own, and her grin was back again. 'So this is what it's all been about . . . I came to Norton Hedley looking for a starship, but this is so much better! A door to Other Worlds!'

'You knew about the ship?' I said.

'I grew up around here, remember? And Black Heir's been trying to find that ship ever since it crashed. I spent years investigating on my own time, so I could sell the location to the highest bidder. When the Organization asked for someone to help research Norton Hedley, I jumped at the chance.' She scowled at Vincent. 'I always was suspicious about you, and all the weird stuff you knew. I was the one who pointed the finger in the official report. When I came back and they told me you'd just died, I couldn't believe it! I went to the mortuary, but your body had already disappeared. And that was all the proof I needed that you weren't what you seemed to be.'

Vincent looked at me. 'Talks a lot, doesn't she?'

'You have no idea,' I said. I turned to Lucy. 'Why were you so keen to keep Penny and me from staying at the Pale Horse?'

'Just keeping you off balance.' She smiled widely, like a vicious child. 'I had you running in circles!'

'Why did you do so much damage to Vincent's cottage?'

'Once I got started, it was too much fun to stop.'

'Why kill the funeral director?'

She shrugged. 'He surprised me while I was searching the place.'

I looked at Vincent. 'Your turn.'

'Why kill Frank and Ellie?' said Vincent.

'They wouldn't answer my questions about you,' said Lucy.

Vincent glared at her. 'They didn't know anything!'

Lucy smiled cheerfully. 'If you'd told them something, they might still be alive. So, really, this is all your fault, isn't it?'

'It never was our ancient enemy,' I said to Vincent. 'Just one mercenary human.'

He didn't take his eyes off Lucy. 'An enemy is an enemy.'

She shrugged easily and turned to me, her eyes sparkling with malice.

'And I was so worried about meeting you . . . With your reputation, I was sure you'd see right through me. But you never suspected a thing!'

'I always knew,' I said. 'Why do you think I sent you away to rummage through Smith's cottage? And when Penny and I went there later, it was obvious that you hadn't been abducted. There was far too much destruction for it to have been any kind of search. And the pool of blood was too small and too neat; it had to have been staged.'

'You think you're so sharp!' Lucy said viciously. 'You still brought me here, right to the big payoff I've been searching for!'

'I wanted you and your weapon a safe distance away from the people in town,' I said calmly. 'And you weren't the only one who followed us through the woods.'

The penny dropped. Lucy had just started to turn when Penny moved in behind her and dropped a hand on her arm, forcing the weapon away from me. Lucy grabbed Penny's arm, bent sharply at the waist and flipped Penny over her shoulder. Penny went crashing to the floor and Lucy backed quickly away, as Penny scrambled back on to her feet. Only to freeze where she was, as Lucy aimed the alien weapon at her. Lucy grinned triumphantly.

'I always knew you were overrated. You get to die first!'

She activated the weapon, and a beam of shimmering light stabbed towards Penny. But Lucy had been distracted just long enough for me to get there first and place my body between Penny and the weapon. The beam hit me square in the chest – and had no effect at all. I nodded easily to Lucy.

'That weapon was only ever designed to work on humans.'

And while Lucy stared at me in shock, I darted forward,

grabbed the weapon out of her hand, broke it in two and threw the pieces away. I stepped back and smiled at Penny.

'Took you long enough to get here.'

She smiled brightly. 'I didn't want to crowd Lucy. But I was here when you needed me – to save the day.'

'At least you waited until I revealed the murderer,' I said.

'It's all in the timing.' She looked at me steadily. 'Were you sure that weapon wouldn't work on you?'

'The old one didn't,' I said. 'I suppose there was always the chance it might have been upgraded.'

'You were ready to die for me.'

'Always.'

'Wait just a minute!' said Vincent. 'You knew all along that she was following us, as well?'

'Of course,' I said. 'You didn't really think I was going to leave her behind, did you? We're partners.'

'Then why the deception?' said Vincent.

'Because I wasn't sure how much I could trust you.'

'Fair enough,' said Vincent.

We all turned to look at Lucy, who glared sullenly at us.

'She killed your friends,' I said to Vincent. 'What do you think we should do with her?'

'You can't kill me!' Lucy said immediately. 'Black Heir would assume the Organization ordered it, and there would be war!'

'Not if you just vanish,' said Vincent. 'A lot of that goes on around here. I am going home . . . and I think you should come with me.'

'You'd let her get away with murder?' I said.

Vincent smiled. 'She won't like where she's going. And she really won't like what the door will make her into so that she can survive there. Are you sure you don't want to come with us?'

'Earth is my home,' I said. 'I belong here.'

'You're not human,' said Vincent.

'I am if I choose to be.' I looked at Lucy. 'I liked Frank and Ellie. And you killed them just because you could. You belong with Vincent. You're as inhuman as he is.'

'What are you talking about?' said Lucy.

'You'll find out,' I said.

The door swung open to show my home world again. Lucy took one look at the alien scene and screamed in horror. Vincent grabbed her by the arm and plunged forward, hauling her through the door. I turned my head away, and so did Penny. Lucy's scream suddenly cut off, and when Penny and I looked again, the open door was showing us the station platform at Norton Hedley.

'I've enjoyed our little chat, sir,' said the caretaker. 'Do feel free to drop by again.'

'Thanks,' I said. 'But I have work to do.'

I walked through the open door on to the platform, and Penny was right there with me. When we looked back, there was no trace of the door anywhere. I took Penny in my arms, and we held each other tightly.

'I had to be sure,' I said. 'I had to see for myself. But I told you I wasn't going anywhere.'

'I never doubted it,' said Penny. 'We're partners.'

'Always,' I said.